AUG -- 2022

FANTASTIC BEASTS

THE SECRETS OF DUMBLEDORE

THE COMPLETE SCREENPLAY

WIZARDING
WORLD

FANTASTIC BEASTS
THE SECRETS OF DUMBLEDORE

THE COMPLETE SCREENPLAY

Screenplay by

J.K. ROWLING & STEVE KLOVES

Based upon a screenplay by

J.K. ROWLING

Foreword by

DAVID YATES

With behind-the-scenes content and commentary from

DAVID HEYMAN, JUDE LAW, EDDIE REDMAYNE, COLLEEN ATWOOD, AND MORE

SCHOLASTIC INC.

Library of Congress Control Number: 2022936957

ISBN 978-1-338-85368-1

10 9 8 7 6 5 4 3 2 1   22 23 24 25 26

Printed in the U.S.A.   37
First edition, July 2022

FOREWORD

D IVING back into J.K. Rowling's Wizarding World with *The Secrets of Dumbledore* was both exciting creatively and challenging logistically, given that production began at the same time as the global pandemic, and we based ourselves for much of it working out of Leavesden Studios in Hertfordshire, England. It was here that Stuart Craig and his exceptional art department team, thwarted by various travel restrictions because of COVID-19, created magical versions of Berlin, Bhutan, and China across the back lot. We also rebuilt some of the most memorable sets from earlier Wizarding World stories and films, including the Hog's Head, the Room of Requirement, and Hogwarts itself.

Jo and Steve's screenplay moves deftly between the old and new while balancing a timely political story with both charm and emotion. At the heart of the tale, one of Jo's most enduring and endearing characters, Albus Dumbledore, deals with present dangers and past regrets, while Newt Scamander leads a mission to prevent Grindelwald's rise to power.

Over many months, as the world fell into a strange hibernation, we worked to translate Jo and Steve's words to the screen.

In *The Secrets of Dumbledore*, dangerous times may favor dangerous men, but the tenacity and the pluck of Dumbledore, Newt, and the gang they assemble to take on the most lethal wizard in over a century holds out the promise that in the end, light and love may yet prevail, however challenging the odds.

—DAVID YATES
March 21, 2022

Warner Bros. Pictures Presents
A Heyday Films Production
A David Yates Film

FANTASTIC BEASTS:
THE SECRETS OF
DUMBLEDORE

Directed by... David Yates

Screenplay by .... J.K. Rowling & Steve Kloves

Based upon a screenplay by .... J.K. Rowling

Produced by .... David Heyman, p.g.a., J.K. Rowling, Steve Kloves, p.g.a., Lionel Wigram, p.g.a., Tim Lewis, p.g.a.

Executive Producers .... Neil Blair, Danny Cohen, Josh Berger, Courtenay Valenti, Michael Sharp

Director of Photography .... George Richmond, BSC

Production Designers .... Stuart Craig, Neil Lamont

Edited by .... Mark Day

Costume Designer .... Colleen Atwood

Music by .... James Newton Howard

STARRING

Newt Scamander .... Eddie Redmayne

Albus Dumbledore .... Jude Law

Credence Barebone .... Ezra Miller

Jacob Kowalski .... Dan Fogler

Queenie Goldstein .... Alison Sudol

Theseus Scamander .... Callum Turner

Eulalie "Lally" Hicks .... Jessica Williams

Tina Goldstein .... Katherine Waterston

and

Gellert Grindelwald .... Mads Mikkelsen

1   INT. TRAIN CAR—DAY

MEN and WOMEN sit silently in the flickering light. CAMERA GLIDES slowly, reveals a MAN standing, strap in hand, gently swaying with the train's movements. His face is hidden to us, but his HAT, set at a mildly rakish angle, is somehow familiar.

2   EXT. STATION—MOMENTS LATER—DAY

The train comes to a halt. The doors open. The men and women stream out, including the man in the hat.

3   EXT. PICCADILLY CIRCUS—MOMENTS LATER—DAY

The man with the hat emerges into the light and separates from his fellow passengers. He glances about briefly, then continues on.

4   INT. CAFÉ—DAY

Busy. Loud. As a WAITRESS with a DARK BOB crosses into view, we go with her, wending as she wends, gracefully gliding to a table near the back, where she sets a cup of something hot in front of the man with the hat: DUMBLEDORE.

(above) **ALBUS DUMBLEDORE COSTUME SKETCH**

(opposite) **PRELIMINARY GRAPHIC FOR ALBUS DUMBLEDORE CASE FILE,
WITH SPACE LEFT FOR MOVING PHOTOGRAPH**

MINISTRY of MAGIC
DEPARTMENT of MAGICAL LAW ENFORCEMENT

FORM NO. 298/7122DY

- AUROR OFFICE · IMPROPER USE OF MAGIC · HIT WIZARDS ·
- WIZENGAMOT ADMINISTRATION SERVICES -

DEPT. OF MAGICAL LAW ENFORCEMENT - CASE FILE

ALL WITCHES AND WIZARDS BEING INVESTIGATED BY THE DEPARTMENT OF MAGICAL LAW ENFORCEMENT UNDER THE JURISDICTION OF THE MINISTRY OF MAGIC ARE SUBJECT TO THE STRICTEST CONFIDENTIALITY, UNTIL OTHERWISE DEEMED NECESSARY BY THE MINISTER FOR MAGIC. THIS FILE IS CONFIDENTIAL AND INFORMATION APPERTAINING TO THIS CASE FILE MUST BE REPORTED BACK TO THE SUPERIOR MINISTERIAL EMPLOYEE OVER SEEING SAID INVESTIGATION.

CASE FILE NUMBER:

ALL INFORMATION REGARDING CASE FILES AND INVESTIGATIVE WORK UNDERTAKEN FOR THE DEPARTMENT OF MAGICAL LAW ENFORCEMEENT IS STRICTLY CONFIDENTIAL.

`0 0 0 8 1 9 1 7 7 X`

NAME OF WITCH OR WIZARD: ALBUS PERCIVAL WULFRIC BRIAN DUMBLEDORE

NATIONALITY: BRITISH

PRESENT ADDRESS: HOGWARTS SCHOOL OF WITCHCRAFT AND WIZARDRY

DATE OF BIRTH: ⚹6/⚹/⊕ᚦ

PROFESSION or OCCUPATION: PROFESSOR OF DEFENCE AGAINST THE DARK ARTS

INVESTIGATIVE NUMBER:
INVESTIGATIVE NUMBER MUST BE CONFIRMED BY SUPERIOR - AS MENTIONED IN ARTICLE 35

`2 X 0 0 0 1 8 ᚱ ᛉ ᚱ`

PHOTO MUST BE RECENT

HEIGHT: 5' 11"
WEIGHT: 175 LBS
COLOUR OF HAIR: FAIR
COLOUR OF EYES: BLUE
COMPLEXION: FAIR

1- R. THUMB | 2- R. MERCURY | 3- R. APOLLO | 4- R. SATURN | 5- R. JUPITER

APPLICANT'S RIGHT HAND FINGER PRINTS - ONLY USE ROYAL PURPLE INK

THE PERSONS MENTIONED BELOW ARE THE KNOWN MEMBERS OF SUBJECTS FAMILY:

SPOUSE: N/A .... BORN AT ....

FATHER: PERCIVAL DUMBLEDORE .. BORN AT.. XX (PLACE) ... XX (DATE)

MOTHER: KENDRA DUMBLEDORE .. BORN AT. XX (PLACE) ... XX (DATE)

SPECIAL PARTICULARS: DESCRIBE ANY MARKS OR SCARS
XXX

KNOWN HISTORY OF SUBJECT (INCLUDING FAMILY HISTORY & EDUCATION)

KNOWN TO HAVE ATTENDED HOGWARTS SCHOOL OF
WITCHCRAFT AND WIZARDRY. SORTED INTO GRYFFINDOR.
FATHER PERCIVAL DUMBLEDORE SENTENCED TO LIFE
IN AZKABAN FOR CRIMES AGAINST MUGGLES.
MOTHER AND SISTER, KENDRA AND ARIANA DECEASED
IN UNKNOWN CIRCUMSTANCES.
DURING ALBUS DUMBLEDORE'S TEENAGE YEARS HE IS
KNOWN TO HAVE MET AND BEFRIENDED THE DARK
WIZARD GELLERT GRINDELWALD.

REASON FOR INVESTIGATION: TICK ALL APPROPRIATE OPTIONS

( ) **KNOWN ILLEGAL ACTIVITIES** ( ) **INFORMANT**
[X] **SUSPECTED ILLEGAL ACTIVITIES**
[X] **OTHER** KNOWN AFFILIATION WITH DARK WIZARD

SECURITY STATUS

CURRENTLY UNDER INVESTIGATION.

in dolorci, at commodo mauris. Sed viverra tempus laoreet. Nam tempor pretium metus id tempus. Proin eleifend felis lorem, eget posuere diam. Praesent p oncus vulput ate. Praesent sit amet neque leo, ac bibendum ligula. Pellentesque vitae eros tellus. Ut et libero nisl. Integer iaculis euismod sem, et adipi molestie ut. Nunc ultricies sem eu massa rhoncus accumsan. Curabitur sed scelerisque justo. Sed nulla ligula, pretium vitae tincidunt a, commodo quis sem habitant morbi tristique senectus et netus et malesuada fames ac turpis egestas. Proin ullamcorper rhoncus nisl vitae dictum. Aenean et pellen tesque s id posuere turpis. Curabitur sed velit nec sapien malesuada eleifend. Phasellus sollicitudin magna quis quam mattis vel porttitor mi adipiscing. Nulla fa sto tellus, ultrices en dictum non, rutrum nec lacus. Aenean viverra fermentum mi, non bibendum libero laoreet vel. Mauris nulla lectus, porta vitae ornar e placerat odio. Vivamus quis tellus arcu, at malesuada risus. Nulla mauris leo, pulvinar sed auctor id, tempor nec turpis. Phasellus fringilla tinci dunta

MINISTRY AUTHORIZATION
C O D E

* ALL INFORMATION IN THIS CASE FILE IS STRICTLY CONFIDENTIAL, AND MUST NOT BE DISCUSSED OUTSIDE OF INVESTIGATORIAL TEAM.

SIGNATURE OF SUPERIOR OFFICER .... DATE ....

PRINTED IN ENGLAND BY THE MINISTRY OF MAGIC PRESS

DUMBLEDORE

Thank you.

WAITRESS

Would you like something else?

DUMBLEDORE

No. Not just yet—I'm waiting.

(*a frown*)

I'm expecting someone.

The waitress nods and turns away. Dumbledore watches her go, then stirs a lump of sugar into his tea, leans his head back, and closes his eyes. We HOLD on him like this, face in repose, for a long time until . . . a LIGHT falls over Dumbledore's face.

Dumbledore opens his eyes, considers the man standing beside his table: GRINDELWALD.

GRINDELWALD

Would this be one of your regular
haunts?

DUMBLEDORE

I don't have any regular haunts.

For a moment, Grindelwald studies him, then sits in the seat opposite.

GRINDELWALD

Let me see it.

Dumbledore stares at him, then slowly brings a hand into view and reveals: the BLOOD TROTH. As he cradles it, its chain slowly slithers between Dumbledore's fingers, as if alive.

GRINDELWALD (CONT'D)

Sometimes I imagine I still feel it around my neck, I carried it for so many years. How does it feel around yours?

DUMBLEDORE

We can free each other of it.

Grindelwald ignores this, glancing about the room.

GRINDELWALD

Love to chatter, don't they, our Muggle friends. Though one must admit: They make a good cup of tea.

DUMBLEDORE

What you're doing is madness—

GRINDELWALD

It's what we said we'd do.

DUMBLEDORE
I was young. I was—

GRINDELWALD
—committed. To me. To us.

DUMBLEDORE
No. I went along because—

GRINDELWALD
Because?

DUMBLEDORE
Because I was in love with you.

They stare into each other's eyes, then Dumbledore looks away again.

GRINDELWALD
Yes. But that's not why you went along.
It was you who said we could reshape
the world, that it was our birthright.

Grindelwald settles back, eyes narrow. INHALES.

GRINDELWALD (CONT'D)

Can you smell it? The stench? Do you
really intend to turn your back on your
own kind for these animals?

Dumbledore's eyes shift, meet Grindelwald's steely gaze.

GRINDELWALD (CONT'D)

With or without you, I will burn down
their world, Albus. There's nothing you
can do to stop me. Enjoy your cup of tea.

*As Grindelwald exits, a LOW RUMBLE begins. Dumbledore
stares down at his teacup, watches it faintly TREMBLE on the
hard surface of the table. As the liquid within QUIVERS, he
seems to get lost in it.*

We go to flames, holding for some time, until we are in . . .

5   INT. DUMBLEDORE'S ROOM—HOGWARTS—MORNING

*We find Dumbledore standing at his window, eyes closed. As
we slowly pull focus to him, his eyes open, and we are back in
the present.*

He holds the blood troth, the chain coiled around his wrist.

WHEN they were teenagers, Dumbledore and Grindelwald came up with this plan for taking control of the wizarding world and beyond, a plan that Grindelwald is now trying to realize. But Dumbledore is a changed man. He understands the mistakes he has made and is trying as best he can to right them. I think that's very potent: We've all made mistakes in our lives, and no matter who we are, we have to acknowledge those mistakes, learn from them, and move on.

—DAVID HEYMAN

(Producer)

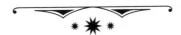

6   EXT. LAKE—TIANZI MOUNTAINS—SAME TIME—NIGHT

A vast, beautiful landscape. Under a low moon, limestone pillars rise majestically out of the water in the shadow of a MOUNTAIN—the Angel Eye.

NEWT paddles across the lake.

7   EXT. TIANZI MOUNTAINS—MOMENTS LATER—NIGHT

Feet delicately step ashore, leaving the bobbing boat behind, and we reveal NEWT SCAMANDER.

Lakes and tributaries fall away behind as he starts an ascent through the bamboo forest.

The distant cry of an animal echoes evocatively across the landscape. Newt listens for a moment. PICKETT, atop Newt's shoulder, listens too.

NEWT
(whispers)

She's ready.

NEWT SCAMANDER COSTUME SKETCHES

WE finally get to see Newt where he's at his best and happiest, which is out in the wild tracking creatures. And in this case it's a very beautiful and extraordinary creature called a Qilin that has this mythical status in the wizarding world. One of the things I've always loved about Newt is that there's this kind of anomaly between his physicality and slight social awkwardness mixed with his dexterity and facility in nature. So it was thrilling when I first saw the script and this almost Indiana Jones–like moment at the beginning of the movie because it's Newt at his most comfortable.

—EDDIE REDMAYNE

(Newt Scamander)

8   EXT. HOLLOW—TIANZI MOUNTAINS—MOMENTS LATER—NIGHT

Newt moves rapidly but carefully toward the mouth of a great cathedral-like cave. As he draws close, something stirs inside, half hidden in shadow.

9   EXT. HOLLOW—TIANZI MOUNTAINS—MOMENTS LATER—NIGHT

Newt tenderly reaches out to stroke the back of the animal as she rolls gently, and we see she's a QILIN: part dragon, part horse, powerful but with a sweetness to her. She's breathing fast, her skin flecking and twitching, insects and bits of jungle and dust caked into her hide.

She lets out another cry.

A GOLDEN LIGHT begins to suffuse the ground beneath her. Newt smiles, entranced. Slowly, slithering out from beneath the mother, a BABY QILIN appears, beautiful and fragile, its eyes blinking blindly. SNIFFING curiously, it softly BLEATS, its tiny body pulsing with GOLDEN LIGHT, briefly illuminating Newt's and Pickett's faces as they peer down at it.

Newt steps back, watches as the mother Qilin licks the baby clean as it shivers and stumbles around.

BABY QILIN SKETCH

NEWT

(off Pickett's look)

Beautiful.

(beat)

Right, you two. Now the tricky bit.

Newt reaches down for his case, opening it gently. We see a photo of TINA pinned inside the lid.

Through the deep undergrowth figures approach, wands being drawn . . .

. . . ACOLYTES ROSIER and CARROW approaching, eyes hungrily on the baby Qilin.

With a WHOOSH Rosier and Carrow raise their wands, firing SPELLS, flaying the mother Qilin's hide. She sways drunkenly, BELLOWING into the night, and then—her legs betraying her—collapses.

IN THE ONSLAUGHT:

Newt sends a defensive spell back and it blooms into a shield, but it's too late.

Glancing back to see a DARK FIGURE emerge between the other Acolytes: CREDENCE, looking older, more assured, as he strikes through Newt's shield with his wand.

COMPARED to Harry Potter or many other heroes from the wizarding world, Newt isn't written as the greatest or most powerful wizard, but he has his own unique facility with magic. So in this fight, rather than just outright dueling spells, Newt uses more organic things, sending leaves into whirlwinds or shields, for example. His magic is not, perhaps, the most impressive, but it feels specific to who he is as a character.

—EDDIE REDMAYNE
(Newt Scamander)

Newt points his wand at his case.

NEWT (CONT'D)

Accio!

The case flies across into his hand.

Credence breaks through the shield as Newt pitches himself over the rim of the hollow, dropping down a treacherous slope as he jumps, stumbles, and trips through the undergrowth.

A THWACK of a spell from behind, splintering BAMBOO around him, SENDS his case tumbling from his hands.

Up ahead we see the baby Qilin standing in the undergrowth, frightened and fragile.

Newt picks up the pace, LOOKS ACROSS TO SEE . . .

. . . legs pop out of the CASE as it bumps and bounces downhill, steering it back toward him.

Carrow jets toward Newt, hands outstretched for the baby Qilin. Newt counters, sending her flying backward.

THWACK! Another SPELL whistles over Newt's head just as he ducks and sweeps his arm around the baby Qilin, scooping

her up, and in that moment another incoming spell HITS HIM and sends him flying off HIGH GROUND AND DOWN.

FROM BENEATH, Newt's body plunges deep into swirling water.

On the foaming surface, Pickett's head pops up, swimming parallel to the shore, WORRIED at the sight of Newt's unconscious body drifting to a stop on the opposite shoreline.

WIDE . . .

. . . to reveal that we are at the base of a series of beautiful, cascading waterfalls that spill down from the Angel Eye.

For a moment, Newt lies in a dreamlike state, blinking up into the sky. Finally, he raises his head.

NEWT'S POV

. . . ZABINI holds a sack while Rosier reaches over and collects the baby Qilin, shoving it roughly into the sack. WHOOSH! In an instant, they are gone.

Newt prizes himself up.

We CUT TO:

. . . Newt stumbling back toward the hollow, one arm wrapped about his case. He reaches the crest of the hollow. The mother Qilin lies in shadow, unmoving. Newt collapses against the mother Qilin's motionless body. His chest heaves painfully.

> ### NEWT (CONT'D)
> I'm so sorry.

Newt squints upward, considering the empty sky. His eyelids grow heavy . . . sleep beckoning . . . his chest rising more steadily . . . when:

His face BLOOMS SOFTLY with light.

His eyes flutter open. The earth beneath him is BLOOMING.

Turning, he studies the mother Qilin, watching as the flesh surrounding her eye TWITCHES and . . .

. . . a SOFT, MURMURING BLEAT breaks the silence. As the LIGHT at his back BLOOMS BRIGHTER, Newt turns, watching as . . .

. . . a SECOND BABY QILIN wriggles into view. As it slips free, it peers around uncertainly, then meets Newt's eyes. Newt smiles before the Qilin wriggles into his arms. He turns back to the mother . . . then stops.

NEWT (CONT'D)
Twins. You've had twins . . .

As he watches, a TEAR trickles from her eye, her PUPIL DILAT-ING. Newt's face falls. He rolls back against the mother's life-less body.

Slowly, Pickett pokes his head out of Newt's pocket, staring at the baby Qilin with wonder.

Newt nods to the case and Pickett hops to, pausing over one of the latches, looking back for guidance.

Still clasping the Qilin, Newt unfastens one latch while Pickett flips open the other.

TEDDY pops his head out, seeing Newt and then looking across at the baby Qilin.

From deep below, in the belly of the case, we follow the leggy limbs of a WYVERN as it climbs upward toward the sky, past the picture of TINA GOLDSTEIN stuck to the inside of the case lid, and then Teddy before emerging UP AND OUT of the case into the Angel Eye itself.

The Wyvern's body starts to expand magically and beautifully before us. With his last bit of strength, Newt gathers the Qilin

close, pulling it within the folds of his coat. Shivering, it bleats softly in his arms.

The tail of the Wyvern wraps around Newt, and he and the baby Qilin are lifted gently into the air.

The Wyvern ascends high into the sky, its great majestic wings expanding gracefully as it carries Newt and the baby Qilin over the expansive waterfalls and toward the horizon, which glimmers faintly with the day's first light.

The TITLE APPEARS:

THE SECRETS OF DUMBLEDORE

10 EXT. CASTLE ENTRANCE/COURTYARD—NURMENGARD—MORNING

We DRIFT, watching Grindelwald leave the castle as the Acolytes Apparate into the far end of the courtyard.

Credence separates from the others.

Grindelwald's eyes are fixed on the sack in Credence's hand. Rosier hovers—silent, watchful. Grindelwald steps forward.

> GRINDELWALD
> Leave us.

The Acolytes withdraw wordlessly. One or two glance back, aware that Credence is now the favorite. Alone with Credence now, Grindelwald nods to the sack.

> GRINDELWALD (CONT'D)
> Show me.

Grindelwald takes the Qilin and peers deeply into its damp eyes. PHLEGM drizzles from its quivering nose.

> CREDENCE
> The others. They said it's special.

> GRINDELWALD
> Oh, it's beyond special. See, see its eyes?
> Those eyes see everything. When a Qilin
> is born, a righteous leader will rise, to
> change our world forever. Her birth
> brings change, Credence, to everything.

Credence eyes the Qilin quizzically.

> GRINDELWALD (CONT'D)
> You did well.

Grindelwald places his hand on Credence's cheek. Credence covers Grindelwald's hand with his own, tentatively, as if unfamiliar with such intimate touch.

GRINDELWALD (CONT'D)

Go. Rest.

11   INT. DRAWING ROOM—SAME TIME—MORNING

QUEENIE watches Credence disappear from view, then returns her attention to Grindelwald, who gently lowers the Qilin to the flagstones, eyeing it with evident fascination.

Reaching out, he gently lifts it to its feet, steadying it, then positions himself in front of it. For a moment, nothing. Then, slowly, the Qilin's head lifts, its weary gaze meeting Grindelwald's expectant one. Then . . .

. . . it turns away. Grindelwald's face hardens. He picks up the Qilin and cradles it in his arms. He reaches into his pocket, something GLIMMERING briefly as he withdraws his hand. Grindelwald's arm rises and . . .

. . . blood spatters the flagstones, the glimmering blade in Grindelwald's hand running red. Queenie's breath catches— almost too softly to hear.

A VISION appears in the pooling blood, of TWO FIGURES, seen from on high, WALKING in the snow.

We CUT TO:

HOGSMEADE LOCATION RENDERING

12 EXT. HOGSMEADE—DAY

Newt and THESEUS trudge through the snow, past TATTY POSTERS of GRINDELWALD—HAVE YOU SEEN THIS WIZARD?

THESEUS
I don't suppose you'd like to tell me
what this is about, would you?

NEWT
He just asked that we meet. And that I be
sure to bring you.

THESEUS
Right.

Theseus studies Newt as they walk ahead into HOGSMEADE.

13 INT. HOG'S HEAD—MOMENTS LATER—DAY

The bearded proprietor (ABERFORTH DUMBLEDORE) runs a dirty rag over the MIRROR behind the bar, his suspicious gaze shifting as Newt and Theseus, in REFLECTION, enter. As they glance about the squalid surroundings, he continues to clean.

ABERFORTH
Here to meet my brother, I expect?

Newt steps forward.

NEWT

We're here to see Albus Dumbledore.

Aberforth eyes them once more in the mirror, then turns.

ABERFORTH

That would be my brother.

NEWT

Oh. Sorry, um . . . brilliant. I'm Newt
Scamander and this is—

As Newt extends his hand, Aberforth turns away.

ABERFORTH

Up the stairs. First on the left.

*Newt stands with his hand extended another moment, then
nods and turns back to Theseus, who raises his eyebrows.*

THE HOG'S HEAD LOCATION RENDERING

14 INT. UPPER ROOM—HOG'S HEAD—CONTINUOUS—DAY

> DUMBLEDORE
> Has Newt told you why you're here?

> THESEUS
> Was he meant to?

Dumbledore eyes Theseus, clocking the mild challenge in his tone.

> DUMBLEDORE
> No, as a matter of fact.

Theseus's eyes shift to Newt, who struggles to hold his gaze.

> NEWT
> There's something we—that,
> Dumbledore—wishes to speak to you
> about. A proposal.

Theseus considers his brother, then Dumbledore.

> THESEUS
> All right.

Dumbledore, having crossed the room, takes the BLOOD TROTH from a table and dangles it in the firelight.

DUMBLEDORE has always been an enigma. He's got this spark, this kind of playful quality to him whilst dealing with ridiculously high stakes. But there's also a kind of slightly father-son, master-apprentice connection between Dumbledore and Newt. In the past movies, Dumbledore's kind of sent Newt out to do his dirty work for him. In this film he's beginning to let him in.

—EDDIE REDMAYNE

(Newt Scamander)

DUMBLEDORE
You know what this is, of course.

THESEUS
Newt had it in Paris. I can't say I have
much experience with such things, but it
looks to be a blood troth.

DUMBLEDORE
That would be correct.

THESEUS
And whose blood is contained within?

DUMBLEDORE
Mine.
(a beat)
And Grindelwald's.

THESEUS
I'm assuming that's why you can't move
against him?

DUMBLEDORE
Yes. Nor he against me.

*Theseus nods, eyeing the troth, watching as the droplets of
blood circle one another like weights in a clock.*

THE SECRETS OF DUMBLEDORE

THESEUS

Can I ask what would possess you to
make such a thing?

DUMBLEDORE

Love. Arrogance. Naivete. Pick your poison.
We were young. We were going to trans-
form the world. This ensured we would.
Even if one of us had a change of heart.

THESEUS

And what would happen if you were to
fight him?

*Newt eyes Dumbledore expectantly, but he remains mute, star-
ing at the troth.*

DUMBLEDORE

It's really quite beautiful, you have
to admit. Were I even to *think* about
defying it . . .

*The blood troth flashes red and flies free, caroming off the floor
and to the wall. As he draws his wand, taking aim, the troth's
chain, still tethered to his arm, constricts, burrowing deep into
his flesh.*

IT'S an interesting time in Dumbledore's life: The man that we all grew to love through the Harry Potter films is not fully formed yet, so we get to see an Albus going through big emotional and life-changing decisions and situations, and all of those lead him to become the much-loved, sage headmaster Albus Dumbledore in later years. So we see him confronting his past, confronting old friends, old foes, and also confronting himself.

—JUDE LAW

(Albus Dumbledore)

As Newt and Theseus look on, Dumbledore begins to approach the troth where it grinds into the wall, a strange smile coming over his face, as if he were in thrall to it.

DUMBLEDORE (CONT'D)

It knows, you see . . .

Dumbledore stares, transfixed. The chain causes the veins in his hand to swell, bulging monstrously. Grimacing, the wand tumbles from his fingers.

DUMBLEDORE (CONT'D)

It senses the betrayal in my heart . . .

Newt's gaze shifts to the DROPS of BLOOD, now circling one another more frantically within the troth.

Dumbledore continues to stare at the troth as it trembles more violently against the wall and the chain snakes slowly up his throat, encircling his neck . . .

NEWT

Albus . . .

. . . drawing tighter, then tighter still . . .

NEWT (CONT'D)

Albus . . .

. . . his eyes rolling up into his head . . .

NEWT (CONT'D)

Albus!

The blood troth drops to the floor and then into Dumbledore's hand, the chain slithering from his neck and reattaching itself to the troth, its host. Gradually the chain loosens and Dumbledore's chest heaves, as if he'd just remembered to breathe. He opens his hand. In his palm, the troth trembles briefly, then goes still.

DUMBLEDORE

That would be the least of it. A young man's magic, but as you can see, powerful magic. It can't be undone.

THESEUS

So this proposal. I take it the Qilin has something to do with it?

Dumbledore's eyes shift to Newt.

NEWT

He promises he won't tell a soul.

Dumbledore turns back to Theseus, answers his question.

DUMBLEDORE

If we are to defeat him, the Qilin is only part
of it. The world as we know it is coming
undone. Gellert is pulling it apart with
hate, bigotry. Things that seem unimagi-
nable today will seem inevitable tomorrow
if we don't stop him. Should you agree
to do what I ask, you'll have to trust me.
Even when every instinct tells you not to.

*Theseus eyes Newt. Finally, he looks up into Dumbledore's
gaze once more.*

THESEUS

Let's hear it.

15 INT. CREDENCE'S ROOM—NURMENGARD—DAY

*Credence's face comes into frame. He meets his own eyes in the
glass, then raises a hand. As he watches, a fly crawls along his
arm. He watches, transfixed, then his eyes shift.*

Queenie stands in the doorway.

CREDENCE

Does he send you? To spy on me?

QUEENIE GOLDSTEIN COSTUME SKETCH

CREDENCE (CONT'D)

QUEENIE

No. But he asks. What you're thinking.
What you're feeling.

CREDENCE

And the others? Does he ask you what
they're thinking and feeling?

QUEENIE

Yes. But it's mostly you.

CREDENCE

And do you tell him?

She starts to reply, then falters. As the veins in his hand lighten, returning to normal, Credence turns, looking at Queenie directly for the first time.

CREDENCE (CONT'D)

You do?

He smiles but there is something unnerving about it.

CREDENCE (CONT'D)

Who's reading whose mind now?
(*smile vanishing*)
Tell me what you see.

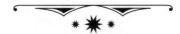

She eyes him, then:

> **QUEENIE**
>
> You're a Dumbledore. It's an important family—you know this because he's told you. He's also told you that they abandoned you, that you were a dirty secret. He says Dumbledore abandoned him too and he knows how you feel. And for that reason . . . for that reason, he's asked you to kill him.

Credence's smile has curdled.

> **CREDENCE**
>
> I want you to go now, Queenie.

She nods, makes to exit, then, at the door, stops.

> **QUEENIE**
>
> I don't. Tell him. Not always. Not everything.

She withdraws, closing the door quietly. Credence stands, unmoving for a moment, then the mirror catches his eye. Slowly, as if drawn by an invisible hand, LETTERS begin to MATERIALIZE on the SURFACE of the glass.

. . . FORGIVE ME . . .

Credence looks unsurprised. Stepping forward, he raises his own hand . . . and wipes the mirror clean.

16 EXT. KOWALSKI'S BAKERY—LOWER EAST SIDE—PREDAWN

A battered metal window shutter RATTLES upward, revealing the sad and lonely figure of JACOB KOWALSKI standing outside in the chill. He stares bleakly within.

17 INT. KOWALSKI'S BAKERY—CONTINUOUS—PREDAWN

The oven door opens to reveal Jacob as he checks that it is still lit.

He grabs a BRISTLED BRUSH and, stepping to the front window, begins to sweep up yesterday's crumbs, chasing off the occasional ROACH.

18 INT. BACKROOM—KOWALSKI'S BAKERY—MOMENTS LATER—
PREDAWN

CLOSE UP—WEDDING CAKE

A blanket of white icing. An ALTAR made of spun sugar. And two TINY FIGURINES: A BRIDE, poised before the altar. The GROOM, lying facedown in a drift of icing.

Jacob delicately takes the groom when—BRINNNG!—the shop BELL sounds. He lays the groom back down on the icing.

19 INT. KOWALSKI'S BAKERY—MOMENTS LATER—PREDAWN

Jacob emerges, apron on his shoulder, stops cold.

> JACOB
> Hey, we're closed—

A WOMAN is peering into the far pastry case.

> JACOB (CONT'D)
> Queenie.

The woman turns, beams. Queenie.

> QUEENIE
> Hi, sweetie.

Jacob approaches.

> QUEENIE (CONT'D)
> Honey, look at your bakery, it's like a
> ghost town.

> JACOB
> Yeah, well, I . . . I . . . missed you.

JACOB KOWALSKI COSTUME SKETCH

KOWALSKI K BAKERY

WE MAKE

BREAD, PASTRIES, CAKES
AND
FANCY CONFECTIONS.

PIERNIK ~ PACZKIS

FAWORKI AKA ~ CHRUST

FROM **2**¢ EACH, OR **4** FOR **6**¢.

BABKA ~ MAKOWIEC

SERNIK ~ BY THE SLICE.

BREADS FROM **5**¢ A LOAF.

INCLUDING

OBWARZANEK KRAKOWSK

CHALLAH ~ ANGIELKA
AND
SLĄSK BREADS.

KOWALSKI BAKERY

443 RIVINGTON STREET. N.Y.

**BREAD, PASTRIES, CAKES
AND FANCY CONFECTIONS.**

WE DELIVER ⏤ ASK IN STORE.

M _____

DATE _____192___

KOWALSKI

K

FANCY
CONFECTIONS
443 RIVINGTON ST.
NEW YORK.

SALESMAN _____

SIGNED _____

THANK YOU FOR YOUR CUSTOM.

(above) **KOWALSKI BAKERY RECEIPT PAD**

(opposite) **KOWALSKI BAKERY PRICE LIST**

Tears well in Jacob's eyes.

> QUEENIE
> Oh, baby. Come here . . . Come here.

She enfolds him in her arms. He closes his eyes.

> QUEENIE (CONT'D)
> Everything's going to be all right.
> Everything's going to be just fine . . .

NEW ANGLE—JACOB HUGGING HIMSELF IN THE EMPTY SHOP

He opens his eyes. Looks at his empty arms. Sighs. Through the grimy front window he catches sight of a shy-looking young woman (LALLY HICKS) sitting on the bus bench across the street.

20   EXT. BUS STOP—LOWER EAST SIDE—CONTINUOUS—PREDAWN

Lally begins to read. In the near distance, we see THREE WORKMEN approaching.

One of the men separates from the others.

WORKMAN 1

Hey, sweetheart. What brings you
downtown?

Lally continues to read her book.

LALLY

I really hope you didn't spend all day
coming up with that.

*The man is a little taken aback by Lally, who remains absorbed
in the book in her lap.*

WORKMAN 1

Oh, you want scary? Is that what you
want?

*The workman waits expectantly as Lally studies him sol-
emnly. Finally:*

LALLY

You know what it is, you just aren't
menacing enough.

WORKMAN 1

I think I'm plenty menacing. Am I not
menacing?

He turns to his two cohorts, who seem uncertain.

> LALLY
> Maybe if you waved your arms around.
> You know, like a crazy man. Then you'd
> appear more menacing.

As the workman continues to gesticulate wildly, Lally leans slightly to her left, peering across the street.

> LALLY (CONT'D)
> That's good, a little more.

21 INT. KOWALSKI'S BAKERY—CONTINUOUS—PREDAWN

Jacob squints, watching as the workman looming over Lally begins to wave his arms.

22 EXT. BUS STOP—LOWER EAST SIDE—CONTINUOUS—PREDAWN

> LALLY
> That's it. Keep going, keep going. Perfect.
> Three, two, one . . .

> JACOB (O.S.)
> *Hey!*

Jacob comes crashing out of the bakery in a cloud of Colonial Girl flour, BANGING the FRYING PAN with a METAL SPOON as he strides across the street. The three workmen circle away from Lally, start toward Jacob.

>   JACOB (CONT'D)
> That's enough. Get outta here . . .

>   WORKMAN 1
> What's on your mind, baker boy?

>   JACOB
> Ah, jeez. You should be ashamed of
> yourselves.

Lally watches carefully as the three men close in on Jacob, never taking her eyes from them.

>   JACOB (CONT'D)
> Tell you what, I'll give you the first shot,
> go ahead—

>   WORKMAN 1
> Are you sure?

BANG!

Workman 1 drops. Jacob freezes. Seconds later the FRYING PAN comes clattering down to earth as he drops it.

The first workman rolls up into a sitting position, rubs his neck.

> **WORKMAN 1**
> Last time I ever help that woman out
> again . . . Lally!

Lally touches her wand to her sad little bob and—in quick succession—her lustrous hair spills forth, the spectacles vanish, and her dowdy dress and stiff collared shirt transform into smartly tailored slacks and a soft, flowing blouse.

> **LALLY**
> Whoopsie, Frank. Sometimes I forget
> my own strength. I'll take it from here.
> Thank you!

> **WORKMAN 3**
> Welcome.

> **WORKMAN 2**
> Catch you later, Lally . . .

> **LALLY**
> Bye, Stanley, I'll be over for a game of
> Befuddler Dudley soon.

WORKMAN 2

All right.

LALLY

That's my cousin Stanley. He's a wizard.

Instantly, Jacob picks up the frying pan and begins to back away, shaking his head.

JACOB

No!

LALLY

Please, it's early, don't make me work for it.

JACOB

I said I wanted out. And I want out.

LALLY

Come now, Mr. Kowalski—

Jacob enters the bakery.

JACOB

My therapist said you wizards don't exist. What a waste of money!

Lally magically appears standing opposite him inside the bakery, chewing on a cinnamon bun.

> LALLY
>
> You do know I'm a witch, right?

> JACOB
>
> Yeah. Look. You seem like a really nice
> witch, but you don't know what I've
> been through with you people—so could
> you please get out of my life.

Jacob opens the door and gestures for Lally to leave. When she continues to talk, he leaves the shop, still carrying the frying pan. Lally follows him.

> LALLY
>
> *(in one long stream)*
>
> A little over a year ago, in the hopes of
> securing a small business loan, you walked
> through the doors of the Steen National
> Bank—located about six blocks from here—
> you then made the acquaintance of one
> Newt Scamander, the world's foremost—
> albeit only—Magizoologist, you then
> learned of a world you had previously
> been wholly unaware of, you met and
> fell in love with a witch named Queenie

Goldstein, had your brain wiped by means
of Obliviation, only it didn't take, and—as
a result—you reunited with Miss Goldstein
who—after your refusal to marry her—
decided to join Gellert Grindelwald and
his dark army of followers, who pose the
single greatest threat to your world and
ours in four centuries. How did I do?

Jacob sits down and just stares.

                    JACOB

Yeah. That's good. Except for the part
about Queenie going over to the dark
side. I mean, yeah, she's cuckoo, but
she's got a heart bigger than this whole
crazy island and she's so smart, she can
legitimately read your brain, she's a
whatchamacallit—

                    LALLY

A Legilimens.

                    JACOB

Yeah . . .

Jacob sighs, stands, and begins to walk toward the bakery.
After a moment, he turns back to Lally.

JACOB

Look. You see this, you see the pan.
(holding up the frying pan)
That's me. I'm the pan. I'm all dented.
Dime a dozen. I'm just a schmo. I don't
know what crazy ideas you have in your
head there, lady, but I'm sure as hell you
can do a lot better than me. Goodbye.

*Jacob turns and hobbles slowly toward the dim lights of
the bakery.*

LALLY

I don't think we can, Mr. Kowalski.

He stops but doesn't turn.

LALLY (CONT'D)

You could've ducked under the counter,
but you didn't. You could've looked the
other way, but you didn't. In fact you
were willing to put yourself in danger to
save a perfect stranger. Seems to me you're
just the kind of average joe the world
needs right now. You just don't know it
yet—that's why I had to show you.
(beat)
We need you, Mr. Kowalski.

Jacob looks at the wedding cake in the bakery and makes his decision. He turns to face Lally.

> JACOB
> All right. Call me Jacob.

> LALLY
> Call me Lally.

> JACOB
> Lally. I gotta lock up.

Lally waves her wand. The door closes, the lights turn out, and the shutters fall over the bakery. Jacob's clothes transform.

> JACOB (CONT'D)
> Thanks.

> LALLY
> Much better, Jacob.

Lally lets the book slip free of her fingers and, boards flapping, it softly flutters in the air, where the pages begin to turn.

As she extends her hand, the pages riffle faster and faster, then explode from the binding, dispersing into the air like a kaleido-scope of butterflies.

LALLY (CONT'D)
I believe you know how this works, Jacob.

As their hands touch, the cyclone of pages descends, engulfing them and—SWOOSH!—they VANISH. Seconds later, the pages flutter back into the binding of the book.

Seconds after that . . . all that is left are a few stray pages that float to the ground.

23 EXT. GERMAN COUNTRYSIDE—DAY

The TRAIN wends through the Brandenburg countryside. We focus in on the CARRIAGE at the tail of the train.

24 INT. MAGICAL TRAIN CARRIAGE—DAY

YUSUF KAMA stands by the window watching the snowy country-side roll past. Newt and Theseus are by a ROARING FIRE, a copy of the Daily Prophet *in Theseus's hand. On Theseus's copy we see:*

ELECTION SPECIAL

Who Will Triumph? Liu or Santos?

Directly below, a pair of PHOTOGRAPHS show the CANDI-DATES themselves: LIU TAO and VICÊNCIA SANTOS.

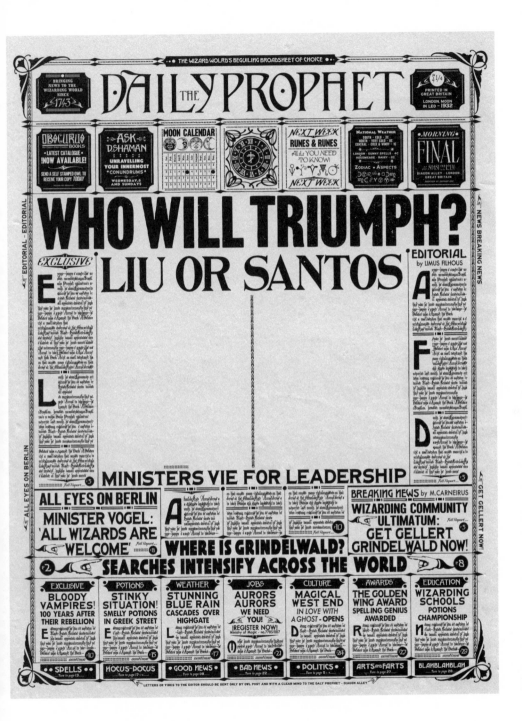

PRELIMINARY GRAPHIC FOR THE *DAILY PROPHET*,
WITH SPACE LEFT FOR MOVING PHOTOGRAPHS OF LIU AND SANTOS

TRAIN INTERIOR LOCATION RENDERING

W E'VE obviously seen the Hogwarts Express a lot in the Potter films, which we've always treated as a real train that Muggles just don't see. The difference here is that they're in a carriage attached to a Muggle train, so we had to move past the concept of a train that's invisible from the outside. When we see the train pull into the station in Berlin and the camera travels from outside to inside, this beautiful carriage is revealed within a tattered baggage car at the end of the train. So it's magically hidden rather than being invisible and that felt more interesting for the world of this film.

—CHRISTIAN MANZ
(Visual Effects)

On the back page, Grindelwald's WANTED poster.

NEWT

What are they saying at the Ministry?
Liu or Santos?

THESEUS

Officially the Ministry takes no position.
Unofficially? The smart money's on
Santos. But *anyone* would be better than
Vogel.

KAMA

Anyone?

Kama's gaze alights on Grindelwald. Theseus clocks it.

THESEUS

I don't believe he's on the ballot, Kama.
He also happens to be a fugitive.

KAMA

Is there a difference?

*Just then, the FIRE SPUTTERS, turning faintly GREEN, and
Jacob stumbles over the hearth. He still holds the frying pan.*

ONE opportunity to really engage with the Art Deco style was the magical train that transports our heroes from London to Berlin. The sculpted panels of the fireplaces are based on some very Art Deco wall decorations. We then took elements of those panels and created the logo for the wizarding train company. Once we've got that as an insignia—and this goes for all insignia across the wizarding world, of the Ministries of Magic, the *Daily Prophet*, and so on—then we can apply it to different media. For example, we created an onboard magazine and tickets for the train, which might not get a close-up, but they help fill that world with all the relevant pieces.

—MIRAPHORA MINA
(Graphic Designer)

(above) TRAIN COMPANY LOGO

(opposite) TRAIN INTERIOR BAS-RELIEF PANEL DESIGN

JACOB

Spinning. Always with the spinning.

NEWT

Jacob! Welcome! You brilliant man. I was
absolutely sure Professor Hicks would
convince you!

JACOB

You know me, pal. Can't pass up a good
Portkey.

*Just then, the grate sputters again and, seconds later, Lally
strides easily out of the fire, clutching the book.*

LALLY

Mr. Scamander?

NEWT

Professor Hicks?

LALLY/NEWT

At long last.

NEWT
(to the others)
Professor Hicks—

(catching himself)
and I have corresponded for many years,
but we've never actually met. Her book on
Advanced Charm Casting is a must-read.

LALLY

Newt is far too kind. *Fantastic Beasts* is
required reading for all my fifth-years.

NEWT

Now, well, let me make introductions.
This is Bunty Broadacre, my indispensable
assistant for the past seven years—

BUNTY

Eight . . .

Two adolescent Nifflers sit on Bunty's shoulders.

BUNTY (CONT'D)

. . . years and a hundred and sixty-four
days.

NEWT

As you can see: indispensable. And this
is—

BOOK COVER DESIGN FOR *ADVANCED CHARM CASTING*
BY EULALIE HICKS

BOOK COVER DESIGN FOR *FANTASTIC BEASTS AND WHERE TO FIND THEM*
BY NEWT SCAMANDER

KAMA

Yusuf Kama. Pleasure.

NEWT

And you've obviously already made
Jacob's acquaintance—

*Theseus CLEARS HIS THROAT. Newt stares blankly at him.
Theseus raises his eyebrows.*

THESEUS

Newt.

NEWT

Oh, yes. Sorry. This is my brother,
Theseus. And he works for the Ministry.

THESEUS

Actually, Head of the British Auror
Office.

LALLY

Ah. Well, I'll have to ensure my wand
registration is up to date.

Lally grins.

THESEUS

Yes. Although, strictly speaking, that
doesn't fall within my purview—

*Newt turns suddenly and walks to the back of the carriage. The
others follow.*

NEWT

All right, then. I imagine you're all
wondering why you find yourselves here.

General consensus all around.

NEWT (CONT'D)

And in anticipation of that, Dumbledore
asked that I convey a message:
Grindelwald has the ability to see
snatches of the future. So we have to
assume that he'll be able to anticipate
what we do before we do it. So if we
hope to defeat him, and to save our
world . . . to save your world, Jacob . . .
then our best hope is to confuse him.

As Newt concludes, he is greeted with . . . silence.

> **JACOB**
> Excuse me? I'm sorry, how do you confuse a guy who can see the future?

> **KAMA**
> Countersight.

> **NEWT**
> Exactly. The best plan being no plan.

> **LALLY**
> Or many overlapping plans.

> **NEWT**
> Thus, confusion.

> **JACOB**
> It's working on me right now.

> **NEWT**
> In fact, Dumbledore asked that I give you something, Jacob.

The others stand by as Newt draws forth from his sleeve—a bit like an amateur magician—a WAND.

> **NEWT (CONT'D)**
> It's snakewood. It's somewhat rare—

JACOB

Are you kidding me right now? Is this
thing *real*?

NEWT

Yes, well, it doesn't have a core, so sort
of—but yes.

JACOB

Sort of real?

NEWT

More importantly, where we're going,
you'll need it.

Jacob takes the wand, stares at it in awe. Newt begins to search his pockets.

NEWT (CONT'D)

Now there's something for you too, I
think, Theseus—

Again, the others wait in anticipation. Newt—truly like a magician this time—tries to draw out something from inside his coat—but something tugs it back. Newt wrestles for a moment, gives it an extra tug, addressing an inside pocket . . .

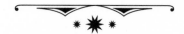

NEWT (CONT'D)

Teddy, please let go. Teddy, please let
go. Teddy. Will you behave. This is
Theseus's . . .

*With a decisive yank, Teddy caroms across the carriage where
he is caught by Jacob. A piece of fabric falls to the floor.*

Jacob and Teddy stare at each other.

*Newt bends down to pick up the piece of fabric. It is a GLITTER-
ING RED TIE patterned with a GOLDEN PHOENIX. He stands
and hands it to Theseus, who takes it and turns it over.*

THESEUS

Well, of course, now everything makes
sense.

NEWT

Lally, Lally, I believe you were given
some reading material . . .

LALLY

You know what they say, a book can
take you around the world and back—all
you have to do is open it.

JACOB
(*popping Teddy down*)
She ain't kidding.

NEWT
Bunty. That's for you. I'm told it's for
your eyes only.

*Newt fishes out a small folded SQUARE of PAPER and hands it
to Bunty. As she opens it, she visibly reacts, but before she can
give it a second read, it catches fire and incinerates.*

NEWT (CONT'D)
Kama—

KAMA
I have what I need.

JACOB
What about Tina? Is Tina coming?

NEWT
Tina's . . . not available. Tina's . . . been
promoted. She's . . . very, very busy.
(*a beat*)
From what I understand.

LALLY

Tina's been made Head of the American Auror Office. We know each other well, she's quite a remarkable woman.

Newt stands for a moment, eyeing Lally, then:

NEWT

She is.

THESEUS

So this is the team that's going to stop the most dangerous wizard we've faced in over a century? A Magizoologist, his indispensable assistant, a schoolteacher, a wizard descended from a very old French family . . . and a Muggle, a baker, with his fake wand.

JACOB

Hey. We got you too, pal. And his wand works.

Jacob knocks back a drink and . . .

THESEUS

True. Who wouldn't like our chances?

D UMBLEDORE chooses people who have a good heart and who have very specific talents. Lally is a renowned Charms professor and she's much admired in the wizarding world. Theseus is Newt's brother and a top man in his field, head of the Auror office in the UK Ministry. Kama, because of his family, has a family history that can be put to use. And why does Dumbledore choose Jacob? Why add a Muggle to this band? Because Jacob has the right moral backbone and is a decent, kind man with a huge, beating heart.

—DAVID HEYMAN

(Producer)

. . . giggles, and we CUT TO:

25 EXT. TRAIN STATION—BERLIN—EVENING

Frigid Berliners stand stiffly on the platform as the train RUM-BLES into the station.

26 INT. MAGICAL TRAIN CARRIAGE—EVENING

Newt, kneeling by his case, finishes feeding the Qilin and gently snaps the case shut.

>   NEWT
> You're all right, little one.

>   LALLY
> Berlin . . . Wonderful.

Newt turns, sees Lally standing by the adjacent window, looking out. One man (TALL AUROR) stands out for both his height and demeanor.

The train ceases its movement, engine HISSING. The others begin to collect their things. Kama is first to the door.

>   THESEUS
> Kama, stay safe.

Kama pauses, locks eyes briefly with Theseus, then nods. As he exits, a CHILL WIND fills the carriage. Bunty appears at Newt's side.

> **BUNTY**
> I must be going too now, Newt.

Newt begins to reply, then stops, looks down, sees that Bunty's hand is entwined with his own on the case's handle.

> **BUNTY (CONT'D)**
> No one can know everything. Not even you.

He looks up at her, but she says nothing more. Finally, he releases the handle.

As she goes, Newt clocks Theseus and Jacob watching him. Turning away, Newt looks back out the window, watching as Kama and Bunty head in opposite directions.

27 EXT. STREET—BERLIN—MOMENTS LATER—NIGHT

A LIGHT SNOW FALLS as Jacob, Newt, Lally, and Theseus move through the street.

> **NEWT**
> Right . . . Well, here it is.

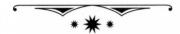

Newt leads them into an alleyway toward a BRICK WALL bearing a CREST. As the others stride toward the wall, Jacob glances from side to side and up and about when . . .

WHOOSH.

. . . the four of them have passed through to the other side. Jacob frowns and sees the same brick wall and the same crest—only depicted from the back.

Shrugging, Jacob looks forward and sees—emblazoned on MASSIVE BANNERS looming over the street—the face of a BENIGN-LOOKING WIZARD (ANTON VOGEL). Farther on, a BUILDING looms, surrounded by SUPPORTERS of Liu and Santos.

THESEUS
The German Ministry of Magic.

NEWT
Yes.

THESEUS
I take it we're here for a reason.

NEWT
Yes. We have a tea ceremony to attend.
And if we don't hurry up, we'll be late.

ONE of the things that I always loved about the Potter films and the whole wizarding world is the idea that we live in our own world and right next door to us, brushing our shoulder through that wall, another more fantastical, more thrilling world exists. Getting to see that in other countries rather than just in London and Britain has been astonishing.

—EDDIE REDMAYNE
(Newt Scamander)

GERMAN MINISTRY OF MAGIC INSIGNIA

GERMAN WIZARDING CURRENCY

GERMAN MINISTRY OF MAGIC ENTRANCE SKETCH

As Newt heads off, Theseus and Lally exchange a glance, then follow. Jacob continues to trip along, glancing about in awe.

> LALLY (O.S.)
> Jacob!

He looks, sees Lally gesturing.

> LALLY (CONT'D)
> Stay with the group.

As Jacob hurries off, he passes a moving WANTED *poster of Grindelwald staring out, following Jacob's every move.*

Jacob can't help but warily hold Grindelwald's gaze.

28 EXT. STEPS—GERMAN MINISTRY—MOMENTS LATER—NIGHT

CONTINGENTS of LIU AND SANTOS SUPPORTERS CHANT and hoist BANNERS in the air in an exuberant but peaceful display of partisan passion. Newt and the others weave their way toward the steps.

As Theseus leads the others through the throng and toward the Ministry entrance, one of the GERMAN AURORS stationed along the perimeter tries to impede Lally and Jacob from ascending the steps.

PRELIMINARY GRAPHIC FOR WANTED POSTER,
WITH SPACE LEFT FOR MOVING PHOTOGRAPHS OF GRINDELWALD

GERMAN MINISTRY OF MAGIC EXTERIOR LOCATION RENDERING

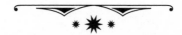

THESEUS

Evening, Helmut.

HELMUT

Theseus.

THESEUS

Hey. They're with me.

The Auror blocking them sees Theseus, and his eyes flicker with recognition. He glances to the COMMANDING AUROR (HELMUT) overseeing all at the top of the stairs, who nods.

Theseus leads the others up.

Just then, the mob surges. Rosier and Carrow are pushing forward through a group of Santos supporters to the concussive beat of drums.

Rosier nods to Carrow, who raises her wand. A bolt of fire strikes a Santos banner. As Santos's face turns to ash, the mood becomes suddenly dark, with much pushing and bumping.

29 INT. GRAND HALL—GERMAN MINISTRY—MOMENTS LATER—
NIGHT

HUNDREDS of DELEGATES mill about while TEAPOTS FLOAT throughout the magnificent room. Theseus walks

alongside Newt, who is glancing about conspicuously, as if searching for someone.

> THESEUS
>
> I take it we're not here for the finger sandwiches?

> NEWT
>
> No. I have a message to deliver.

> THESEUS
>
> A message? To who?

Newt stops. Looking. Theseus follows his gaze.

At the opposite end of the room, Anton Vogel, the benign wizard glimpsed on the STREET BANNERS, presses the flesh while a phalanx of BODYGUARDS shadows his every step, and a FEMALE ATTACHÉ (FISCHER) keeps him moving.

> THESEUS (CONT'D)
>
> You are joking.

> NEWT
>
> No.

As Newt heads in their direction, Theseus follows and we CUT TO:

NEW ANGLE—JACOB AND LALLY

> JACOB
> What are we even doing here? Let's
> go outside. I'm not very good in these
> situations.

> LALLY
> These situations?

> JACOB
> With all the people. The fancy people.

> EDITH
> *Hello!*

Jacob jumps, finds an elderly matron (EDITH) on his elbow.

> EDITH (CONT'D)
> I saw you enter the room and I thought
> to myself, "Edith, that's an interesting-
> looking man."

> JACOB
> (nervous)
> Jacob Kowalski. How are you? Very nice
> to meet you.

> **EDITH**
> And where is it that you hail from, Mr. Kowalski?

> **JACOB**
> Queens.

> **EDITH**
> Ahhh.

Edith nods slowly and we CUT TO:

NEW ANGLE

Newt, trailed by Theseus, approaches Vogel and his contingent.

> **NEWT**
> Herr Vogel, I wonder if I could have a word—

Vogel turns at the sound of Newt's voice.

> **VOGEL**
> Merlin's beard! It's Mr. Scamander, isn't it?

> **NEWT**
> Herr Vogel . . .

The bodyguards loom. Theseus looms. Vogel stares long at Newt, then waves his hand, signaling the bodyguards to stand down. As they step aside for privacy, Newt leans close.

> NEWT (CONT'D)
> I have a message from a friend. And it cannot wait. *"Do what is right. Not what is easy."*

Newt straightens. Vogel remains still.

> NEWT (CONT'D)
> He said it was important that I reach you tonight. That you hear them, tonight. The words.

Fischer appears.

> FISCHER
> It's time, sir.

> VOGEL
> *(ignoring her)*
> Is he here? In Berlin?

Newt hesitates, not sure how to respond.

VOGEL (CONT'D)

No. Of course not. Why leave Hogwarts
when the world outside is burning?

(frowning)

I thank you, Mr. Scamander.

As Fischer spirits Vogel away, she glances back at Newt.

*The sound of a SPOON AGAINST CHINA cuts through the chatter
and all eyes turn to Fischer, standing with a teacup in hand, Vogel
at her side. Once she has the room's attention, she steps aside and
Vogel takes the stage. The audience applauds as he steps forward.*

VOGEL (CONT'D)

Thank you, thank you. I see many
familiar faces here tonight.
Colleagues, friends, foes . . .

As the crowd CHUCKLES.

VOGEL (CONT'D)

Within the next forty-eight hours, you—
along with the rest of the wizarding world—
will choose our next great leader. A choice
that will shape our lives for generations to
come. I have little doubt that no matter who
should triumph, the Confederation will be
in able hands. Liu Tao. Vicência Santos.

ELECTION BANNER DESIGNS FOR CANDIDATES LIU AND SANTOS

As Vogel gestures to Liu Tao and Vicência Santos, who we recognize from the Prophet, *those present APPLAUD.*

> VOGEL (CONT'D)
> It's at moments such as these we are
> reminded that it is this peaceful transfer
> of power that marks our humanity and
> demonstrates to the world that, despite
> our differences, all voices deserve to be
> heard.

Vogel looks off. Theseus, watching from a few yards away, tracks his gaze. One after another, BLACK-CLAD AURORS are staging themselves at each exit.

> VOGEL (CONT'D)
> Even voices which many may find
> disagreeable.

Theseus tracks Acolytes walking through the room.

> THESEUS
> Newt, any of those lot look familiar to you?

Newt follows Theseus's gaze.

> NEWT
> Paris. The night that Leta . . .

THESEUS

They were with Grindelwald.

Theseus tracks Rosier through the crowd. She looks back, almost taunting him to follow. He follows, trying to reach her, and Newt follows at a distance.

VOGEL

And so, after an extensive investigation, the Confederation has concluded that insufficient evidence exists to prosecute Gellert Grindelwald for the crimes against the Muggle community of which he was accused. He is hereby absolved of all his alleged crimes.

Newt registers what Vogel's said. Suddenly, the room explodes in response: outrage, scattered cheers, confusion.

JACOB

Are you kidding me? They're letting the guy off? I was there! He was killing people!

A knowing hardness comes over Lally's face. Then:

THESEUS

You're under arrest! All of you! Wands down!

Theseus, wand raised, is in a tense standoff with five Dark Aurors.

A SPELL hits Theseus in the neck and he drops. Helmut appears, the tip of his wand smoking.

> **HELMUT**
> Nehmen Sie ihn weg.

Two Aurors lift Theseus.

Newt wheels and moves through the crowd in shock, as if shot himself.

> **NEWT**
> Theseus! Theseus!

As Newt breaks through the crowd, Lally and Jacob arrive at his side.

> **LALLY**
> Newt, Newt. Not here. Newt, we don't
> stand a chance.

Calmly, Helmut turns, as does the phalanx of Dark Aurors behind him.

LALLY (CONT'D)

Let's go. Newt. They have the German
Ministry. We've got to go.

*Jacob shouts back into the room as he gets caught in the
mass exodus.*

JACOB

It ain't right . . . it ain't right. That's not
justice . . . extended investigation . . .
Were you there . . . I was there . . . you
let a killer off!

Lally grabs hold of him.

LALLY

We have to go! We have to go! Jacob,
let's go!

*The ROAR of the CROWD RISES. A BANNER of Grindelwald
unfurls above the throng encircling the Ministry. The crowd
begins to CHANT Grindelwald's name, their voices growing
LOUDER and LOUDER, and we CUT TO:*

UTTER SILENCE

SNOW FALLS LIKE SUGAR

THROUGH A DARK SKY

THE HOG'S HEAD EXTERIOR LOCATION RENDERING

30 EXT. HOGSMEADE—NIGHT

*The storefronts are shuttered. The street a long white blanket.
Pristine.*

31 INT. UPPER ROOM—HOG'S HEAD—SAME TIME—NIGHT

*Dumbledore stands before the PAINTING of ARIANA. It's as if
she's watching him.*

32 INT. HOG'S HEAD—SAME TIME—NIGHT

*Dumbledore and Aberforth sit across from each other in the
empty pub, eating. Their spoons dipping into the bowls in front
of them is the sole sound for a time.*

> DUMBLEDORE
> *(the soup)*
> That's very good.

Aberforth continues to eat.

> DUMBLEDORE (CONT'D)
> Her favorite. Remember how she begged
> Mother to make it—Ariana— Mother
> claimed it calmed her. I think that was
> wishful thinking—

PORTRAIT OF ARIANA DUMBLEDORE

ABERFORTH

Albus.

Dumbledore stops, sees his brother looking him in the eye.

ABERFORTH (CONT'D)

I was there. I grew up in the same house.
Everything you saw, I saw.
(a beat)
Everything.

Aberforth tucks back into his soup. Dumbledore studies his brother, burdened by the distance between them, then begins to return to his own bowl when—suddenly—a RAPPING is heard. Aberforth CALLS OUT GRUFFLY:

ABERFORTH (CONT'D)

Read the sign, you stupid sod!

Dumbledore looks toward the FAMILIAR SHADOW beyond the entrance, rises.

33 INT./EXT. PUB ENTRANCE—MOMENTS LATER—NIGHT

Dumbledore pulls open the door: MINERVA McGONAGALL.

MINERVA McGONAGALL

I'm sorry to disturb you, Albus—

DUMBLEDORE
Tell me, what is it?

MINERVA McGONAGALL
It's Berlin.

34 INT. HOG'S HEAD—CONTINUOUS—NIGHT

Aberforth sits, listening to McGonagall's and Dumbledore's MURMURING VOICES, then—as if sensing something—turns.

The SURFACE of the GRIMY MIRROR behind the bar is SHIM-MERING ODDLY.

Rising slowly, Aberforth crosses the room and stares into the mirror. Over his own bleary REFLECTION, WORDS EMERGE, as if rising to the surface of a pond:

DO YOU KNOW WHAT IT'S LIKE

Aberforth considers the message for a moment, then seizes a nearby oily rag to wipe the mirror clean.

35 INT./EXT. PUB ENTRANCE—MOMENTS LATER—NIGHT

McGonagall kneads her hands fretfully. Dumbledore's face is serious, contemplating what he's just been told.

> DUMBLEDORE
>
> I'm going to need someone to cover my morning classes, can I impose on you?

> MINERVA McGONAGALL
>
> Of course. And, Albus. Please be . . .

> DUMBLEDORE
>
> I'll do my best.

McGonagall starts to exit, stops, CALLS OUT.

> MINERVA McGONAGALL
>
> Evening, Aberforth.

> ABERFORTH (O.S.)
>
> Evening, Minerva. Apologies for calling you a stupid sod.

> MINERVA McGONAGALL
>
> Apology accepted.

McGonagall turns away then, and Dumbledore shuts the door.

36 INT. HOG'S HEAD—CONTINUOUS—NIGHT

Aberforth, hearing his brother's footsteps, turns away from the mirror to see Dumbledore carrying his hat and coat.

> DUMBLEDORE
> I'm afraid I'll have to cut our evening short.

> ABERFORTH
> Off to save the world, are we?

> DUMBLEDORE
> That will take a better man than me.

Dumbledore shrugs on his coat, then stops, his gaze fixing on the mirror, watching as the words **DO YOU KNOW WHAT IT'S LIKE TO BE ALONE** *slowly appear. As he looks away, he sees Aberforth staring at him.*

> ABERFORTH
> Don't ask.

The brothers stand like this, eyes locked on each other, then Dumbledore exits. Aberforth listens to him go, then glances once more into the words in the mirror.

37 EXT. COURTYARD—NURMENGARD CASTLE—SAME TIME—NIGHT

The glowing PHOENIX sweeps through the air to catch a crust of bread. Credence stands below, his face suffused with a quiet joy as he watches it.

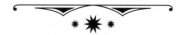
38 INT. DRAWING ROOM—NURMENGARD CASTLE—SAME TIME—
NIGHT

Grindelwald stands at a large window. As he watches the Phoenix, a vision of Dumbledore surfaces on the glass, then slowly gives way to Kama. He studies it, eyes fixed, when Rosier appears.

> ROSIER
> There are thousands in the streets.
> Chanting your name. You're a free man.

Grindelwald nods.

> GRINDELWALD
> Tell the others to prepare to leave.

> ROSIER
> Tonight?

> GRINDELWALD
> Tomorrow. We'll have a visitor in the morning.

Through the window, the Phoenix comes briefly into view, shedding ash. Grindelwald peers down into the courtyard where Credence stands.

ROSIER

Why does it stay with him?

GRINDELWALD

It must sense what he's about to do.

ROSIER

And you're sure? That he can kill
Dumbledore?

GRINDELWALD

His pain is his power.

Rosier looks at Grindelwald.

39 INT. GERMAN MINISTRY OFFICE—CONTINUOUS—MORNING

*Newt, Lally, and Jacob chase a MINISTRY OFFICIAL down
a corridor.*

NEWT

The man that I'm inquiring about is the
Head of the British Auror Office! How
can you have misplaced the Head of the
British Auror Office!

The official, turning to face him, stares placidly at Newt.

MINISTRY OFFICIAL

It's our contention that since he
was never in our custody, we never
misplaced him.

LALLY

Sir. There were dozens of people there.
Any one of them can corroborate—

MINISTRY OFFICIAL

And your name is?

The official looks into Lally's eyes when:

JACOB

Let's get out of here . . . Hey! Wait!
That's the guy—

*Newt and Lally turn. Through the glass corridor, Helmut can
be seen emerging from an office in the company of the Tall
Auror we first saw on the train platform.*

Jacob gestures for the official to follow him.

JACOB (CONT'D)

Come here! Come here!

Jacob, Lally, and Newt rush to the door.

JACOB (CONT'D)
JACOB (CONT'D)
Excuse me! Hey! That's the guy. He knows
where Theseus is. Hello! Where's Theseus!

Helmut continues walking, ignoring them all.

JACOB (CONT'D)
That's him—he knows about Theseus.

Suddenly, a sheet of glass slides down from above like a guillotine.

40   EXT. GERMAN MINISTRY—MOMENTS LATER—MORNING

As Newt, Jacob, and Lally slip out of a side entrance, Lally stops.

LALLY
Newt.

*Newt and Jacob look back, see a GLOVE floating in midair.
The GLOVE points around the corner. Newt walks forward and
catches the glove in his hand. Then, following a second glove,
Newt approaches a figure behind a pillar. Dumbledore.*

41   EXT. GERMAN MINISTRY—MOMENTS LATER—MORNING

*Recovering one glove from the air and taking the second from
Newt, Dumbledore leads the others briskly down a busy avenue,*

his eyes constantly moving, as if every shadow offered the possibility of threat.

> NEWT

Albus.

> DUMBLEDORE

Theseus has been taken to the Erkstag.

> NEWT

But the Erkstag shut down years ago.

> DUMBLEDORE

Yes, well, it's the Ministry's secret little
bed-and-breakfast now. You'll need this to
see him . . . and one of these . . . and this.

Dumbledore places both gloves into his hat as he removes some PAPERS and slips them to Newt, clocking Newt's look.

Dumbledore leads them to the wall and they head through it. Lally pushes Jacob, who appears reluctant.

> JACOB

Wait, wait, wait!

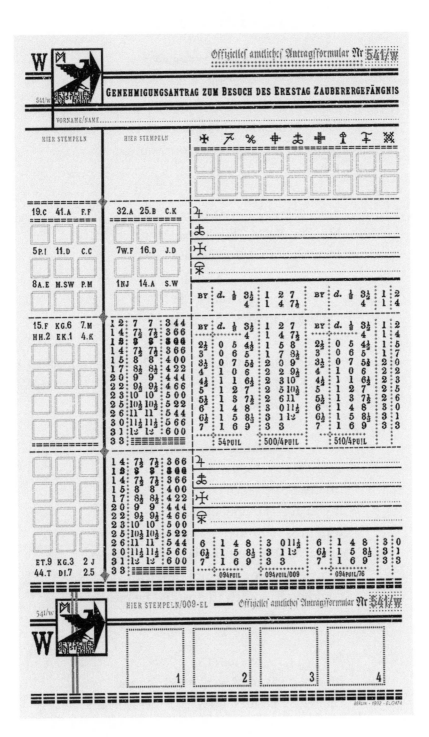

ERKSTAG VISITOR APPLICATION FORM

DUMBLEDORE (CONT'D)

I trust you're enjoying your wand, Mr. Kowalski?

JACOB

Me. Oh. Yeah. Thank you, Mr. Dumbledore. It's a real pip.

DUMBLEDORE

I advise you to keep it close.

As Jacob ponders the meaning of this, Dumbledore fishes a POCKET WATCH from his coat and angles it. Newt sees Credence slide over the REFLECTION inside the lid.

DUMBLEDORE (CONT'D)

Professor Hicks, assuming you're not otherwise engaged—and frankly, even if you are—I'd encourage you to attend tonight's Candidates' Dinner. Take Mr. Kowalski. I'm quite certain there will be an assassination attempt. Anything you could do to scotch that would be greatly appreciated.

LALLY

It's my pleasure. I shall welcome the challenge. Besides, I'll have Jacob with me.

Jacob, having monitored this conversation, looks mildly alarmed. Dumbledore clocks it.

> DUMBLEDORE
> Not to worry, Professor Hicks's defensive
> magic is superb. Until next time.

He smiles, doffs his hat, and exits.

> LALLY
> Such a flatterer.
> *(a beat)*
> Well, not really. It is superb.

Newt steps forward, calls out.

> NEWT
> Albus!

Dumbledore turns, looks back.

> NEWT (CONT'D)
> I was just wondering . . .

Newt gestures as if holding a case.

> DUMBLEDORE
> Ah, yes. The case.

NEWT

Yes.

DUMBLEDORE

(continuing on)

Rest assured it's in safe hands.

42   EXT. BERLIN STREETS—MOMENTS LATER—LATE MORNING

Bunty—Newt's case in hand—skirts a tram and steps briskly across the street to a LEATHER GOODS store.

43   INT. OTTO'S LEATHER GOODS—SAME TIME—LATE MORNING

As a SMALL BELL tinkles, OTTO, a large, wispy-haired MAN in an apron, looks up from a table cluttered with shears and mallets and clamps.

OTTO

Can I help you?

Bunty steps to the counter and places Newt's case carefully on the glass top.

BUNTY

Yes. I'd like to have this case replicated, please.

BUNTY BROADACRE COSTUME SKETCH

OTTO

Certainly.

Bunty watches nervously as the man runs his calloused hands over the beaten case, examining it from myriad angles, then tries to flip open the catch.

BUNTY

Oh, no. You mustn't open it! I mean, that's not necessary. The interior isn't important.

The man eyes Bunty curiously, then shrugs.

OTTO

I see no reason I can't make you one.

As the man turns to get paper and pen on the shelf behind, the baby Qilin pops her head out of the case and peers around curiously. Bunty quickly—and gently—eases her back inside just before the man turns back.

OTTO (CONT'D)

If you leave it here—

BUNTY

Oh, no. I couldn't. Leave it. And I'll be needing more than one. You see, my

husband he's a bit absentminded. He's
always forgetting things—just the other
day he forgot he was married to me. Can
you imagine?

She laughs, a bit maniacally, realizes it, and composes herself.

> BUNTY (CONT'D)
> But I love him.

> OTTO
> Exactly how many were you thinking?

> BUNTY
> Half a dozen. And I'll need them in two
> days' time.

44 EXT. BERLIN STREETS—MOMENTS LATER—LATE MORNING

Bunty returns across the street holding Newt's case.

45 INT. CREDENCE'S ROOM—NURMENGARD CASTLE—LATE MORNING

*Queenie peers down. Sees Zabini and Carrow in defensive
posture.*

> ZABINI
> *Show your hands!*

A FIGURE calmly raises his hands, continues to advance . . .

46 EXT. COURTYARD—NURMENGARD CASTLE—SAME TIME—LATE
MORNING

The figure takes a few more steps. Stops. Kama. Zabini separates from the others and crosses to him.

                    ZABINI
          Who are you?

                    KAMA
          My name is Yusuf Kama.

Grindelwald and Rosier emerge from the castle.

                    GRINDELWALD
          Who's our visitor?

                    KAMA
          I'm an . . . *admirer.*

                    ROSIER
          You murdered his sister. Her name was Leta.

Grindelwald eyes him.

YUSUF KAMA COSTUME SKETCH

KAMA

Leta Lestrange.

GRINDELWALD

Ah, yes. You and your sister share an
ancient bloodline—

KAMA

Shared. It's the only thing we shared.

Grindelwald studies Kama carefully.

GRINDELWALD

Dumbledore sent you, am I right?

KAMA

He fears you are in possession of a
creature. He fears the use you may put it
to. He sent me here to spy on you. What
would you like me to tell him?

GRINDELWALD

Queenie. Is he telling the truth?

Queenie eyes Kama. Something troubles her eyes.

She nods.

Grindelwald's gaze shifts to Credence in the shadows. Grindelwald nods, almost imperceptibly, and Credence slips away. Grindelwald turns his gaze back on Kama.

GRINDELWALD

What else?

QUEENIE

Even though he believes in you, he holds
you responsible for his sister's death. He
carries her absence with him every day.
Every breath he takes is a reminder that
she breathes no more.

Queenie sees Kama staring into her eyes. Grindelwald nods to himself, as if pondering this. Then draws his wand.

GRINDELWALD

Then I presume you won't mind if I
relieve you of your sister's memory.

Grindelwald steps forward and places the tip of his wand to Kama's temple, watching him, to see if he will resist in any way. But Kama remains still, stalwart.

GRINDELWALD (CONT'D)

Right?

KAMA

Right.

Slowly, Grindelwald retracts his wand, extracting a TRANSLU-CENT STRAND as he does. Queenie attempts to remain composed, watching as—for a fleeting moment—a sense of loss ripples through Kama's face.

Just then, the translucent strand breaks free of Kama's temple. It flutters like a kite's tail at the end of Grindelwald's wand and then turns to MIST.

GRINDELWALD

There. Better?

Kama stares ahead, eyes unfocused. Finally, Kama nods.

GRINDELWALD (CONT'D)

I thought so. When we allow ourselves
to be consumed by anger, the only
victim is ourself.
              (a smile, then:)
Now. We were just about to depart.
Perhaps you'd like to join us? Come, we
can talk some more about our mutual
friend, Dumbledore.

Queenie watches Grindelwald begin to escort Kama inside, when—just as he passes—Kama's vacant eyes meet hers—briefly aglimmer with intensity—as if he were sending her a message. As he vanishes inside:

ROSIER

After you.

Queenie looks up, sees Rosier studying her. Rosier gestures and closes the door behind her as we CUT TO:

47 EXT. CROWDED STREET—BERLIN—DAY

Dumbledore, walking briskly, heads through the Berlin streets. Credence follows behind.

Dumbledore crosses the street and slowly comes to a stop in front of a shop, where he sees Credence, in the reflection of the window, visible behind and between passing cars.

Dumbledore slowly blows on a snowflake, and it transforms into a water droplet.

We follow the drop as it flies into the window like a translucent bullet and over the reflected view of the trams and cars, traveling across to Credence, breaking on his forehead. As it bursts, the sound of the street melts away, becoming distant.

DUMBLEDORE

Hello, Credence.

Dumbledore turns and faces him. Credence tenses, wand ready, as Dumbledore steps out into the street. The world around them seems different, slower somehow, like we have shifted into a subtle mirror of BERLIN, a reflection of itself.

They circle each other; the crowds around them seem oblivious. Credence, wand poised.

CREDENCE

Do you know what it's like? To have no one? To always be alone?

Dumbledore slowly realizes.

DUMBLEDORE

It's you. You're the one sending messages in the mirror.

CREDENCE

I'm a Dumbledore. You abandoned me. The same blood that runs my veins runs yours.

The PHOENIX swoops past; Dumbledore glances up at it. The dark energy emanating from within Credence starts to ripple outward, cracking the pavement, lifting the tram rails up

around them. Dumbledore studies the energy, recognizing it, all the while the world around seems to continue on as normal.

CREDENCE (CONT'D)
He's not here for you. He's here for me.

The ground starts to splinter and break around Credence. Dumbledore tenses, sensing what may be coming.

A GREEN BOLT spits from Credence's wand. Dumbledore parries it, his movements smooth, wicked-fast. Instantly, Credence advances and fires another spell, lifting the ground and smashing it forward around Dumbledore, who dissipates the explosive onslaught before he Apparates out of the way.

Credence is running now, lifting cars, masonry, glass from windows, all collecting and sending a rippling, seismic earthquake ahead of him, toward Dumbledore.

Before Dumbledore can parry any further, Credence is upon him, the two locked arm in arm as they duel.

Behind them, a TRAM is approaching and Dumbledore Apparates backward. Credence follows, and we go with them ONTO THE TRAM, as Credence seeks him out in his relentless onslaught. Credence releases another powerful spell, splitting THE TRAM IN HALF, as we travel at blinding speed from INSIDE OUT AND BACK INTO the street with them.

SILENCE

The STREET, eerily quiet now, and for the first time, Credence starts to register how the world around him feels different.

Credence, suddenly aware of a wand at his neck, turns to see Dumbledore standing behind him.

Dumbledore lifts the DELUMINATOR.

> **DUMBLEDORE**
> Things are not quite what they appear,
> Credence. No matter what you've been
> told.

With a flick, the STREET around them is sucked into it, melting like a painting, leaving a negative image of the real world as if it were a distant memory.

> **CREDENCE**
> My name is Aurelius.

> **DUMBLEDORE**
> He's lied to you, to kindle your hate.

Credence, frustrated, lashes out, lightning fast, and for a moment, he and Dumbledore duel at kinetic speed.

USUALLY if we smash up a city, we then have to fix it. But here Dumbledore and Credence are in a mirror world, and that gives us the chance to really show off Credence's unique skills as a wizard and come up with new ways to visualize spells, which ultimately are like these beautiful sculptures in the air. One thing we did was experiment with changing matter, so what looks like it should be solid becomes a liquid, or a massive tsunami of rubble becomes snow with the flick of a wand. And in the end, we're left in this world that's gone completely black, but in the melted puddles all over the ground you can see daylight and traffic in the real Berlin going on just as it was.

—CHRISTIAN MANZ
(Visual Effects)

Dumbledore defends easily when Credence fires a VOLLEY of EXPLOSIVE SPELLS, which Dumbledore weathers before he stretches out his hand and hits Credence with a spell that sends him reeling backward, causing a black, kinetic mass to erupt from his body.

Gently lowered by Dumbledore's hand, Credence falls slowly, his back on the snowy street, staring upward at the angry sky, at the circling Phoenix.

Dumbledore, chest heaving, lowers his wand and as the black vapors writhe behind Credence, watches the Phoenix swoop down, hover briefly over Credence, then beat its wings and soar off.

NEW ANGLE—CREDENCE

Dumbledore approaches. He crouches down—calmly—watching at Credence's side.

Credence's eyes shift, peer into Dumbledore's.

> **DUMBLEDORE (CONT'D)**
> What he's told you isn't true. But we
> do share the same blood. You are a
> Dumbledore.

Hearing this, Credence's eyes meet Dumbledore's. They remain like this for a moment, connected, before the flowing black

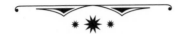

mass rushes back into Credence. Dumbledore gently places his hand on Credence's chest.

DUMBLEDORE (CONT'D)
I'm sorry for your pain. We didn't know,
I promise.

Dumbledore lifts the DELUMINATOR once more, a spell ripples forth, and he and Credence are now in the street, the world of their duel reflected beneath them in pools of water collected by the melted snow.

Dumbledore steps back from Credence, studying him carefully, and stretches out his hand.

When Credence takes it, Dumbledore reaches down and lifts him up, before slipping away into the busy street. Credence watches him go.

48 EXT. CLOSED U-BAHN ENTRANCE—BERLIN—SAME TIME—
EVENING

We see Newt approach and unlock a RUSTED GRILLE.

49 INT. ERKSTAG PRISON—BERLIN—MOMENTS LATER

A GUTTERING CANDLE eerily illuminates an unkempt WARDER stationed before a wall of PIGEON HOLES.

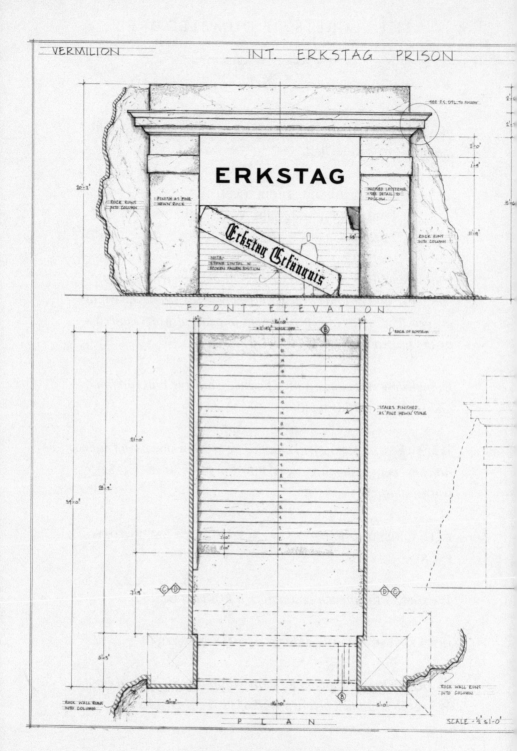

ERKSTAG

Erkstag Gefängnis

F R O N T   E L E V A T I O N

P L A N

SCALE - ½" = 1'-0'

ERKSTAG PRISON ELEVATION

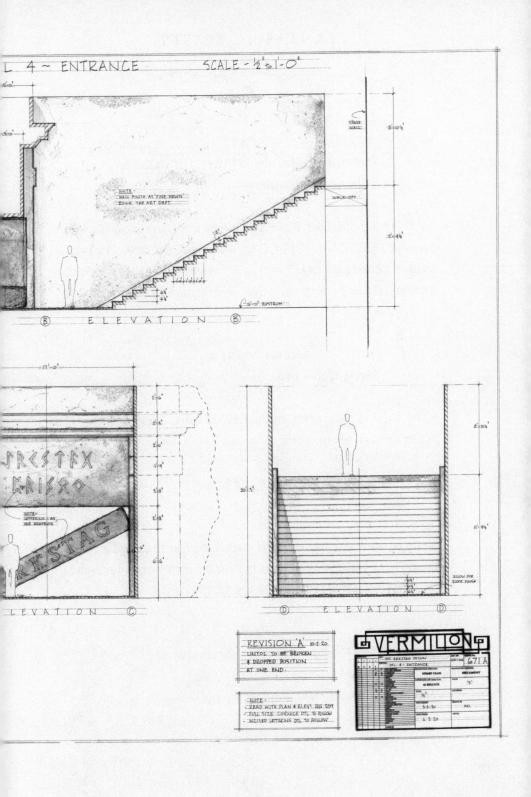

L 4 ~ ENTRANCE   SCALE - ½" to 1'-0"

STAGE
WALL

NOTE
WALL FINISH AS 'FINE HEWN'
ROCK. SEE ART DEPT.

WALK-OFF

B   E L E V A T I O N   B

17'-0"

2'-6"

4'-6"

2'-0"

4'-8"

3'-0"

4'-3"

6'-6"

NOTE
LETTERING AS
PER GRAPHICS

SRCSTFX
ERISRO

RKSTAG

ALLOW FOR
FLOOR FINISH

L E V A T I O N   C   D   E L E V A T I O N   D

REVISION 'A' 10-2-20
LINTOL TO BE BROKEN
& DROPPED POSITION
AT ONE END.

NOTE
- READ WITH PLAN & ELEV'S. DRG 389
- FULL SIZE CORNICE DTL TO FOLLOW
- INCISED LETTERING DTL TO FOLLOW

VERMILION

	MRS. BERKSTAG DESIGNS		671A
	DTL. 4. ENTRANCE		
	STEWART CRAIG	NEIL LAMONT	
	AL BULLOCK		
	½"		
	3-2-20		
	6-2-20		

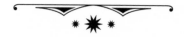

NEWT

I've come to see my brother. His name is
Theseus Scamander—

*As Newt extends the PAPERS Dumbledore provided, a well-
traveled PHOTOGRAPH of Tina spins onto the desk. An over-
zealous charmed STAMP moves its way across Newt's papers,
heading toward the photograph. Newt snatches it away just
in time.*

NEWT (CONT'D)

Sorry, that's just . . .

*Newt then notices: The Warder is wearing Theseus's tie. He
stares for a moment, then:*

WARDER

Wand.

*Newt frowns, reaches into his coat, reluctantly complies. The
Warder rises stiffly and begins to pass his own wand over Newt.
As it hovers over a pocket, a SQUEAK is heard.*

NEWT

Oh. That's— I'm a Magizoologist . . .

The Warder fishes Pickett out of the pocket.

NEWT (CONT'D)
He's perfectly harmless. He's just a . . .
pet, really.

Pickett cranes his neck upward and frowns.

NEWT (CONT'D)
Sorry.

Teddy pokes his head out of another pocket.

NEWT (CONT'D)
That's Teddy—he's a total nightmare,
truth be told—

WARDER
They stay here.

Reluctantly, Newt hands both over, watching miserably as the Warder places Pickett, along with Newt's wand, into one cubby-hole and Teddy into another, his plump body filling it to capacity. Pickett SQUEAKS BESEECHINGLY.

With a SICKENING, SQUELCHING SOUND, the Warder plunges his hand into a BUCKET SQUIRMING with GRUBS, plucks one out, and shakes it in his fist, where it QUIVERS briefly before transforming into a FIREFLY. He deposits it in a tiny tin LANTERN. As it flutters about, the lantern glows feebly

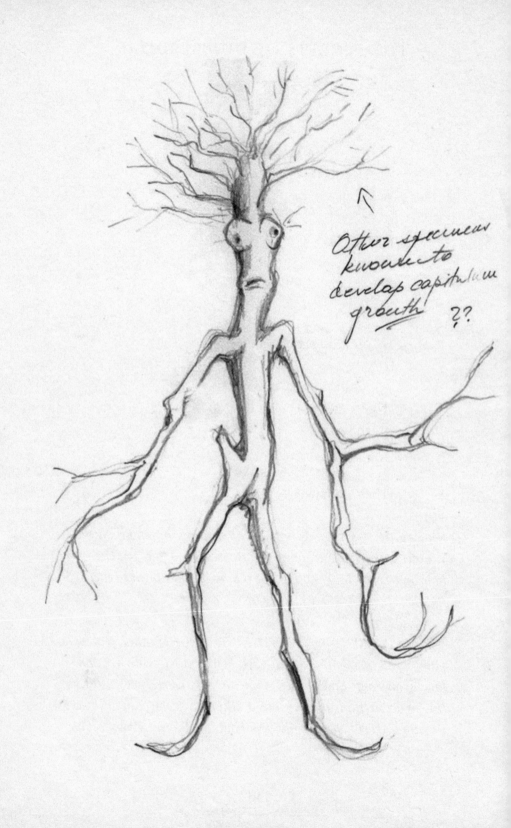

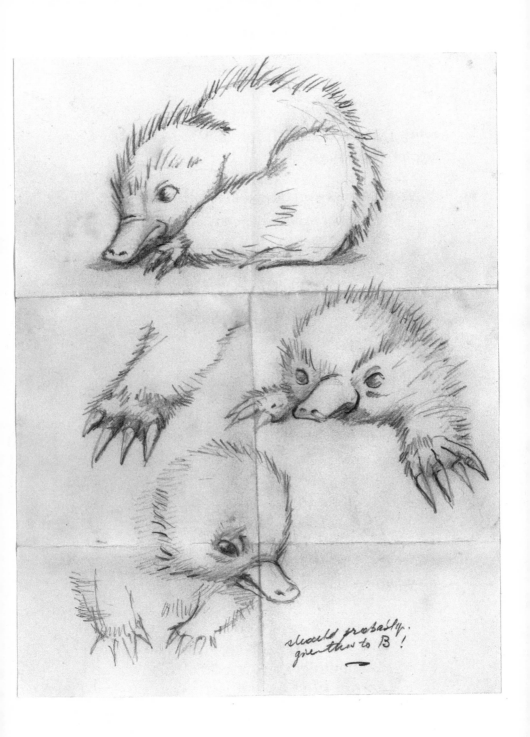

NEWT SCAMANDER NOTEBOOK SKETCHES

with a TREMULOUS LIGHT. Taking the lantern in hand, Newt eyes the dark passage.

> NEWT
>
> How will I know where to find him?

> WARDER
>
> He is your brother?

> NEWT
>
> Yes.

> WARDER
>
> He will be the one who looks like your brother.

As Newt heads off, Pickett stares after him.

> NEWT
>
> I'll be back, Pick. On my word.

Just before the darkness swallows him, Newt looks back.

> WARDER
>
> "I'll be back, Pick. On my word." And I'll be Minister of Magic one day.

The Warder GRINS CRUELLY. Teddy looks on as Pickett sticks out his tongue at him.

50 EXT. GERMAN MINISTRY—NIGHT

The streets surrounding the Ministry are now teeming with supporters of Grindelwald, holding placards bearing his likeness as the DRUMMERS beat their skins fiercely. At the top of the steps, Helmut surveys it all impassively.

51 INT. GRINDELWALD'S CAR—CONTINUOUS—NIGHT

Grindelwald stares—with cool fascination—at the FUNHOUSE OF FACES beyond the tinted glass. Rosier sits beside him.

The faces beyond are no longer in focus. Instead, an IMAGE plays on the glass, an image only Grindelwald can see. Jacob bearing a wand.

Rosier has leaned forward and is talking to the driver.

> **ROSIER**
> Take us around back. It's not safe here.

> **GRINDELWALD**
> *(coming round)*
> No. Roll it down.

GELLERT GRINDELWALD MONOGRAM HOOD ORNAMENT DESIGN

ROSIER

What?

GRINDELWALD

The window. Roll it down . . .

Hand trembling, Rosier reaches out and CRACKS the window.
Instantly CLAWING FINGERS probe the shadows of the car

and VOICES RAGE. Throughout, Grindelwald remains calm, eyes shut. Then, without warning, he LIFTS the door latch . . .

> ROSIER

No! No!

As Grindelwald pitches himself into the maelstrom outside, Rosier sits frozen.

52 EXT. GERMAN MINISTRY—CONTINUOUS—NIGHT

Waving like a Roman magistrate, Grindelwald lets the tide of rabid supporters sweep him up the steps.

53 INT. BALCONY ABOVE—GERMAN MINISTRY—SAME TIME—NIGHT

A TALL BRITISH WITCH stands with the FRENCH MINIS-TER (VICTOR), Fischer, and Vogel, staring down at the swelling crowd.

> VOGEL

Those people aren't *suggesting* we listen to them. They aren't *asking* us to listen. They're *demanding* it.

> BRITISH WITCH

You're not actually proposing that man be allowed to stand—

FOR THE
GREATER
GOOD

VOTE

Gellert
GRINDELWALD

GRINDELWALD ELECTION MATERIALS

VOTE
Gellert

GRINDELWALD

FOR
SUPREME MUGWUMP

INTERNATIONAL
CONFEDERATION
OF WIZARDS

BEHOLD THE INSIGNIA OF THE GREATER GOOD

VOGEL

Yes! Yes, let him stand!

Below, Rosier, white as a ghost, steps out of the car and watches Grindelwald move through the crowd.

BRITISH WITCH

Gellert Grindelwald wants Muggle-
Wizard war! And if he gets his wish,
he won't just destroy their world, he'll
destroy ours as well.

VOGEL

Which is why he cannot win! Let him
stand as a candidate. Let the people vote.
When he loses, the people will have
spoken. But deny them their voices . . .
and those streets will run with blood.

The others look down, watch Grindelwald borne over the arms of the crowd and up the steps of the Ministry.

54 INT. PASSAGEWAY—ERKSTAG PRISON—NIGHT

A tiny fluttering blob of light approaches. As it draws closer, Newt comes clear. He stops.

NEWT

Theseus!

Tiny movements can be heard in the surrounding shadows.

Newt crouches, swings the lantern. A tiny crab-like creature—a BABY MANTICORE—scuttles into view. Seeing Newt, it waggles its antennae. It is—there's simply no denying it—adorable.

Newt seems less than charmed. As he watches, another baby Manticore appears, then another, then another still. One peers up, bares TEETH. Not adorable.

Newt backs away into a central atrium, his feet at the edge of a great pit. He looks down into the vast, dark hole. Something stirs in the shadows below.

Newt suddenly adopts an odd, crab-like pose. The baby Manticores copy him.

55 INT. GRAND HALL—GERMAN MINISTRY—NIGHT

Plates of lobster are being ferried to tables. Seated now, Lally's eyes rake the room, clocking the tables where Liu and Santos sit and assessing the potential threat the BUSBOYS and WAITERS orbiting them pose. One DARK-EYED WAITER keeps crossing into Lally's view.

As Jacob's GOBLET magically fills with wine, he takes it and—noticing Edith waving enthusiastically from across the room—tips his goblet in a toast. He then notices a DISTINGUISHED WIZARD with conductor's hair sitting to Edith's left.

JACOB

Lally. The guy with the hair. Sitting
next to Edith. He looks like he can kill
somebody. He also looks like my uncle
Dominic.

LALLY

(looking)

Is your uncle Dominic the Norwegian
Minister of Magic?

JACOB

No.

LALLY

Didn't think so.

Lally smiles. Then, abruptly, the energy in the room shifts and Grindelwald and his entourage stumble into the room in high spirits. Hair askew, jacket rumpled, Grindelwald seems rakishly authentic in this room of wheezing wannabes. He turns to the HOUSE ELF QUARTET to resume playing.

JACOB KOWALSKI COSTUME SKETCH

He moves through the room, trailed by Rosier, Queenie, Kama, Carrow, Zabini, and Acolytes.

As Queenie crosses, Jacob rises.

> JACOB
> Queenie . . . Queenie.

Queenie knows he's there but blanks him completely.

> GRINDELWALD
> *(spotting Santos)*
> Madam Santos. A pleasure. Your
> supporters are in fine voice.

> SANTOS
> *(a steely smile)*
> As are yours, Mr. Grindelwald.

Grindelwald constructs a smile.

56 INT. FAR PASSAGEWAY—ERKSTAG—NIGHT

Theseus hangs from his ankles in a small cell. As a CLATTER-ING SOUND RISES, he peers down the passageway, watching as Newt comes into view, doing an odd sidelong scissor walk, trailed by HUNDREDS of BABY MANTICORES, all of whom appear to be mimicking him.

THESEUS

Rescuing me, are you?

NEWT

That's the general idea.

THESEUS

(Newt's scissor walk)

I presume this—whatever it is that you
are doing—is strategic?

NEWT

It's a technique called limbic mimicry.
It discourages violent engagement.
Theoretically. I've only actually
attempted it once before.

THESEUS

And the results?

NEWT

Inconclusive. Also, that was a laboratory
setting and the conditions were strictly
controlled, and the current conditions
are more volatile, making it less
predictive of ultimate outcome.

NEWT is not a social animal. He is much more at ease with his creatures. He's not inherently someone that's good at being part of the system and he didn't really fit in at school. In fact, he ended up being thrown out! Whereas Theseus is very much the schoolboy hero who's gone into a life within the Ministry, was a war hero himself, and has a physical authority and a facility with people that Newt just doesn't have. So they're sort of chalk and cheese and yet because in this movie they have to work together they begin to realize that actually they complement each other quite well.

—EDDIE REDMAYNE
(Newt Scamander)

THESEUS

Ultimate outcome presumably being our
survival.

Newt remains very still as a huge ANTENNA emerges from the darkness below. Theseus and Newt stare at each other in alarm. Newt delicately turns to the antenna, it studies him for a moment, then the lamplight in the cell adjacent to Theseus's sputters out.

The antenna retreats down and a giant, scorpion-like tail plunges into the now-dark cell, retrieving the cocooned body that's in there and pulls it down into the pit below. A beat. Then:

The body is CATAPULTED back up from the darkness, landing with a SLOPPY THUD feet away. Newt raises his lantern to reveal it's been disemboweled, food now for the horde of Manticores that tumble over to feast. Newt grabs his moment and sidles into the cell, clawing away at the fibrous yarn encasing Theseus's ankles.

Newt claws the last remaining strands, and Theseus drops to the ground.

THESEUS (CONT'D)

Well done.

The brothers step out of the cell to face a further ocean of Manticores, blocking their exit.

> THESEUS (CONT'D)
> And the plan is?

> NEWT
> Hold this.

He passes his lantern to Theseus. He cups his hands and emits an ODD WHISTLE akin to a whippoorwill.

57 INT. ERKSTAG PRISON—SAME TIME—NIGHT

As the Warder SNORES, feet up, Pickett unlocks the padlock on his cubbyhole and opens the door.

58 INT. ERKSTAG—SAME TIME—NIGHT

> THESEUS
> What the bloody hell was that for?

> NEWT
> We're going to need some help.

Newt strikes a BALLETIC limbic mimicry pose. The baby Manticores immediately copy him.

IN the Erkstag sequence, the whole thing is lit by these lanterns that each contain a glow-fly. And the story is that the Manticore really doesn't like those bugs, so they're hung outside everybody's cell. When a lantern goes out, the Manticore attacks. So as soon as you see your bug die, you know you're dead, because the Manticore will come and skewer you.

—CHRISTIAN MANZ
(Visual Effects)

NEWT (CONT'D)

Follow me.

(a beat)

Come on.

Theseus assumes the same position, and Newt and Theseus start to shuffle away.

NEWT (CONT'D)

You're not swiveling properly. Swivel, swivel, but delicately.

THESEUS

I'm swiveling like you're swiveling, Newt.

NEWT

I don't believe you are.

Between them, a second LAMP outside a cell entrance goes out, and the tail comes up and takes another body.

After a beat, it too is deposited sloppily at their feet. Theseus and Newt share a look.

THESEUS

Swivel.

59 INT. GRAND HALL—GERMAN MINISTRY—NIGHT

Queenie sits quietly. A TEAR trickles from her eye, tracking down the side of her face no one at the table can see.

Across the room, Jacob stares intently at her. We HOLD on them, lost in each other, the surrounding world irrelevant and fading, until . . .

GRINDELWALD

Go to him.

Queenie jumps, finds Grindelwald leaning close. He nods over her shoulder to where Credence lingers near the entrance. Queenie rises . . .

GRINDELWALD (CONT'D)

Queenie. Tell him it's all right. I can see
he's failed. He'll have another chance.
It's his loyalty I most value.

Grindelwald's eyes are locked on hers. She nods and, disengaging from him, heads off.

NEW ANGLE—LALLY

Lally watches Queenie cross the room. Jacob stands as she passes by, but Queenie, steeling herself—we can see it's hard for her now—blanks him again. Jacob, crushed, sits once more.

Lally looks over to Grindelwald. Rosier enters the room with the Dark-Eyed Waiter. The Dark-Eyed Waiter pauses, then moves toward Santos's table.

Lally starts to track the Dark-Eyed Waiter's journey across the room with a glass of ruby-red liquid. Tossing her napkin down, Lally rises and turns to Jacob as she goes.

LALLY

Stay here.

Jacob gulps another glass of wine.

Lally pushes past waiters and picks her way through busboys.

LALLY (CONT'D)

Apologies.

Lally watches the Dark-Eyed Waiter draw closer to Santos . . .

. . . the Dark-Eyed Waiter leans over Santos, setting the glass down. Lally approaches but is stopped by two bodyguards.

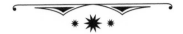

JACOB

Oh boy . . .

Jacob approaches Grindelwald's table like a man on a swaying ship.

As Santos raises her glass, the ruby-red liquid rises into the air menacingly. Lally discreetly sends a spell, and the liquid hovering above Santos's glass zooms down the high table and hits a door, corroding the wood.

As Jacob arrives at the table, Grindelwald, only just now aware of him, eyes him mildly.

JACOB

Let her go.

GRINDELWALD

Excuse me?

Jacob draws his wand.

NORWEGIAN MINISTER

Assassin!

Lally turns, looking back in disbelief as Jacob now holds up both hands.

WHOOSH! Lally flicks her wand again, and Jacob's arm holding the wand is thrust vertically into the air. A tornado-like VORTEX consumes the room, as if the contents of the room were tossed in a blender.

Lally quickly sends another spell, tying the bodyguard's shoelaces together.

Guests flee as each and every chandelier is TREMBLING and the draperies are billowing along the wall, the tablecloths are pitching to and fro, and napkins are taking flight like doves.

A FIGURE can be sensed—a suggestive BLUR—in the distance beyond. As Jacob's eyes adjust, we RACK FOCUS and see the FIGURE is . . .

Queenie.

She stands much like him, still amidst the chaos, staring at him. Their eyes lock. . .

. . . as Queenie begins to slip from view, pulled on by Kama.

Helmut and his Aurors enter the room.

Queenie, just before vanishing, FLICKS her own wand and sends a chair careening toward Helmut, temporarily obscuring his view of Jacob.

Lally pulls out her book and flips it into the air. She drops a chandelier on Helmut and his Aurors as the pages cascade forth, causing a series of steps to appear. Jacob turns and takes them at pace as Lally rushes toward him on the pages, firing spells at the Aurors.

Helmut shoots a fiery blast, setting the steps alight as Jacob rushes toward Lally. WHOOSH! They are sucked into the book.

60 INT. ERKSTAG PRISON—SAME TIME—NIGHT

The Warder SNORTS, his chair tipping backward. Teddy—one end of the glittering necktie clenched in his teeth—skates forward, the pads of his tiny feet SQUEAKING across the surface of the desk.

Above, Pickett precariously balances on the edge of one of the cubbyholes, trying to retrieve Newt's wand.

BELOW, as the Warder wakes, the chair steadies. Then . . .

It falls back as the knot in the tie is finally pulled undone and the Warder crashes like a tree that's been felled, SMASHING into the cubbyholes and launching Pickett forward.

Teddy leaps up, ignoring Pickett in midair, and grabs some falling coins before crashing to the ground.

The WHISTLE echoes again.

61 INT. CELLBLOCK—ERKSTAG—SAME TIME—NIGHT

The lamplight in Theseus's hand is frittering in and out. We hear a crunch, and Theseus stops.

The baby Manticores suddenly pause, staring. Theseus looks down and slowly, delicately, lifts his right foot, under which we see a squashed baby Manticore.

He looks at Newt.

In that instant, the light in Theseus's lamp fizzles out, plunging them both into darkness and sending the baby Manticores running away.

The HUGE tail lifts up, starts to recoil to strike.

As one, the brothers bolt, the tail smashing into the cell walls feet away from them.

Newt and Theseus race through corridors, the Manticore's tail and antennae whipping, SNAKING, smashing, and sending fiery bolts after them, followed by the GIANT MANTICORE itself, squeezing through crevices, close in pursuit.

Theseus swings right and races precariously along a ledge as the Manticore ferociously bears down upon him. Eyes, claws,

limbs of the beast flail toward him, before Theseus trips left, just avoiding the limb that has almost skewered him.

Newt and Theseus reunite and rush forward as the ceiling collapses behind them, trapping the Giant Manticore.

Theseus breathes a sigh of relief just before one of the Manticore's antennae snakes around his waist and drags him away. Newt desperately follows, grabbing at his brother.

Racing toward them is Teddy—Theseus's tie clenched in his teeth, Pickett riding atop like a cowboy—carrying Newt's wand. The Warder fires spells after them before hitting Teddy and causing Pickett to be jettisoned forward into the air with Newt's wand.

Newt holds on to Theseus as he is pulled toward the edge of the pit by the Giant Manticore. Pickett lands at his feet with his wand.

Newt sees him, retrieves his wand, and Pickett quickly grabs hold. Newt casts a spell toward Teddy . . .

NEWT

Accio!

. . . who is lifted into the air and tumbles toward them.

NEWT (CONT'D)

Grab the tie!

They begin to tumble into the pit.

. . . And they are gone.

The Warder chuckles to himself until his lamp starts to flicker and extinguish. He looks out in alarm into the inky darkness.

62 EXT. WOODED AREA—CONTINUOUS—NEXT MORNING

Newt and Theseus crash down through a thicket and land heavily on mossy ground. Covered in leaves, they rise, still holding hands.

Theseus pushes the Manticore antennae from his waist. It slithers toward the lake.

NEWT

That was a Portkey.

Theseus hands Teddy, still clinging to the tie, to Newt.

THESEUS

Yeah.

NEWT

(to Pickett and Teddy)

Well done, you two.

Newt and Theseus emerge from the trees and look across a shimmering lake. A CASTLE rises beyond. Teddy and Pickett peer out of Newt's pocket. Pickett COOS with delight.

Hogwarts.

Above the castle, a QUIDDITCH PLAYER pursues a GOLDEN SNITCH.

63 INT. GREAT HALL—HOGWARTS—MOMENTS LATER—MORNING

Lally sits with a few students finishing breakfast.

LALLY

Not that either of you asked but I would highly recommend learning charms.

Newt and Theseus walk in.

NEWT

Lally.

LALLY

What kept you two?

HOGWARTS EXTERIOR LOCATION RENDERING

> **NEWT**
> We encountered some complications.
> And you?

> **LALLY**
> We encountered some complications.

She hands Newt the Daily Prophet. *Theseus peers over Newt's shoulder. On the front page is a PHOTOGRAPH of Grindelwald and Jacob under a SCREAMING HEADLINE:*

MURDEROUS MUGGLE!

> **THESEUS**
> Jacob tried to murder Grindelwald?

> **LALLY**
> It's . . . a long story.

Jacob sits at a House table with a group of students. He is showing them his wand.

> **REDHEADED RAVENCLAW**
> Is it really snakewood?

> **JACOB**
> Yes, it's really snakewood.

• THE WIZARD WORLD'S BEGUILING BROADSHEET OF CHOICE •

DAILY THE PROPHET

BRINGING NEWS TO THE WIZARDING WORLD SINCE 1743

£1/4 · PRINTED IN GREAT BRITAIN · LONDON, VENUS IN PISCES · 1932

BREAKING NEWS - BERLIN SPECIAL - BREAKING NEWS

MURDEROUS MUGGLE!

EXCLUSIVE

EDITORIAL by LIMUS FILHOUS

MURDEROUS MUGGLE!

NEWS BREAKING NEWS

MAYHEM AT GERMAN MINISTRY OF MAGIC
GRINDELWALD ESCAPES ATTACK

GRINDELWALD ESCAPES ATTACK

BREAKING NEWS by M.CARNEIRUS
LIU TAO AND VICÊNCIA SANTOS UNITED AGAINST GRINDELWALD

UNITED AGAINST GRINDELWALD

MUGGLE'S FANTASTICAL ACCOMPLICES!

EXCLUSIVE
BRAZILIAN WIZARDS
ENCHANT THE EUROPEAN WIZARDING COMMUNITY

continue 10

POTIONS
WARDOUR ST SCANDAL!
FRENCH POTION-MAKER TRAPPED IN THE ATTIC

continue 15

1
2
3

MOON CALENDAR

ASK D.SHAMAN · UNRAVELLING YOUR INNERMOST CONUNDRUMS · WEDNESDAYS AND SUNDAYS

NATIONAL WEATHER
SOUTH · VERY COLD · 3ℭ
NORTH · VERY COLD · 1ℭ
CENTRAL · COLD & WINDY · 4ℭ
LONDON · RAINY · 7ℭ
HOGSMEADE · RAINY · 1ℭ
ZODIAC · ASPECTS

NEXT WEEK ELECTION SPECIAL · ALL YOU NEED TO KNOW! · NEXT WEEK

MORNING FINAL · DIAGON ALLEY · LONDON · GREAT BRITAIN

• SPELLS · Turn to page 13 ....
HOCUS-POCUS · Turn to page 6 ....
• GOOD NEWS · Turn to page 09 ....
• BAD NEWS · Turn to page 22 ....
• POLITICS · Turn to page 5 ....
ARTS and FARTS · Turn to page 27 ....
BLAHBLAHBLAH · Turn to page 28 ....

PRELIMINARY GRAPHIC FOR THE *DAILY PROPHET*, WITH SPACE LEFT FOR MOVING PHOTOGRAPH OF JACOB KOWALSKI

FANTASTIC BEASTS

A TINY SECOND YEAR WITCH leans close.

TINY WITCH
Can I . . . ?

She begins to reach out toward the wand.

JACOB
Uh-uh. It's very dangerous—it's very powerful. It's rare, if it got in the wrong hands— you know, it could mess you up.

WITCH
Where did you get it?

JACOB
I got it for Christmas.

LALLY (O.S.)
Jacob! Look who I found.

Jacob turns to see Lally, Newt, and Theseus.

JACOB
Hey! It's my wizard friends.
(to the kids)
Newt and Theseus. We're like this.

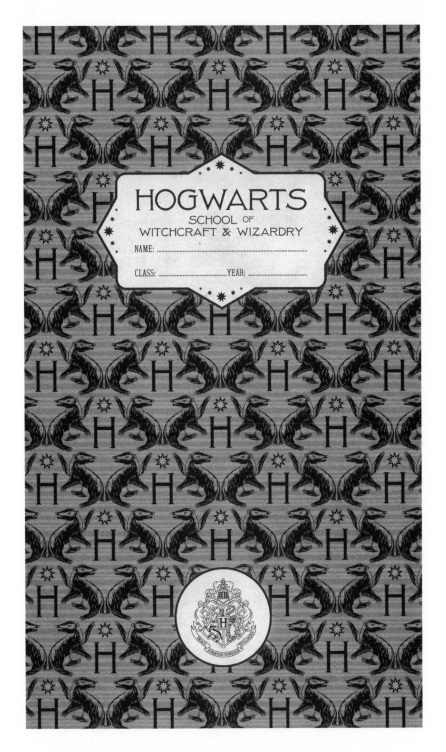

HUFFLEPUFF NOTEBOOK COVER DESIGN

Jacob crosses his middle and forefinger and sticks out his thumb.

JACOB (CONT'D)

And that's me right there. I gotta go.
All right, have fun. Don't do anything
I wouldn't do.

As Jacob and the others come together.

JACOB (CONT'D)

Can you believe this place, they got
pint-sized witches and wizards running
around here.

THESEUS

Uh. You don't say?

JACOB

(to Newt)

I was the assassin.

LALLY

Newt and Theseus both went to
Hogwarts.

JACOB

Oh. I knew that. Well, they're being
very nice to me. The Slytherin boys

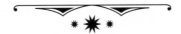
over there, they gave me these. They're
delicious, who wants one?

*Jacob takes a packet from his pocket and tips a DARK CLUMP
into his mouth, offers it to the others.*

NEWT
I never cared for cockroach clusters
much myself. Though Honeydukes are
supposed to be the best.

*As Jacob blanches, a COLLECTIVE BURST OF LAUGHTER
rises from the Slytherins. They proceed to the back of the Hall.
The others turn to see McGonagall, who ushers students away.
Dumbledore approaches.*

THESEUS
McGonagall. Albus.

DUMBLEDORE
Well done. All of you. Well done.
Congratulations.

THESEUS
Congratulations?

I THINK Hogwarts is the place that Dumbledore feels most at home. It's his sanctuary from the world.

—JUDE LAW
(Albus Dumbledore)

IN this film, Dumbledore is looking a little more refined than we've seen him previously, particularly with regard to materials and fabrics. The tweediness of his costumes conveys the idea of luxury and comfort, and the very soft grays hearken to the lavender that he wears later in the Potter films.

—COLLEEN ATWOOD
(Costume Designer)

ALBUS DUMBLEDORE COSTUME SKETCH

PRELIMINARY GRAPHIC FOR *TRANSFIGURATION TODAY* FRONT PAGE

DUMBLEDORE

Indeed. Professor Hicks managed to foil an
assassination. And you are alive, and you
are well. The fact that everything did not
go precisely to plan, was precisely the plan.

LALLY

Countersight 101.

THESEUS

Albus. Forgive me, but aren't we back
where we started?

DUMBLEDORE

Actually, I would argue that things are a
great deal worse.
(to Lally)
You haven't told them, have you?

Theseus and Newt turn to Lally.

LALLY

Grindelwald has been allowed to stand
in the election.

THESEUS/NEWT

What! How?

DUMBLEDORE
Because Vogel chose easy over right.

Dumbledore sweeps his wand into the air, etching together IMAGES of hand-drawn MOUNTAINS and VALLEYS as though he were a street artist. The images start to MATERIAL-IZE out of smoke all around them and then slowly transform into a beautiful landscape. The others stare up in wonder.

Jacob looks around, disoriented.

THESEUS
It's all right.

NEWT
Bhutan.

DUMBLEDORE
Correct. Three points to Hufflepuff.
The kingdom of Bhutan sits high in
the Eastern Himalayas. It's a place of
indescribable beauty. Some of our most
important magic has its origins there.
They say if you listen carefully enough,
the past whispers to you. It also happens
to be where the election will be held.

THE SECRETS OF DUMBLEDORE

CLOUDS *form under the Hall's ceiling. Amidst them an EYRIE can be glimpsed, visible one moment, gone the next.*

THESEUS
He can't win, can he?

DUMBLEDORE
Only a few days ago he was a fugitive
from justice. Now he's an official
candidate in the International
Confederation of Wizards. Dangerous
times favor dangerous men.

Dumbledore turns and begins to make his way back down the Great Hall. The image of Bhutan begins to fade away into smoke behind him.

The others stare after him.

DUMBLEDORE (CONT'D)
And by the way, we'll be dining with my
brother in the village. Should you need
anything before then, Minerva is here.

As Dumbledore exits, Lally leans in, speaks quietly.

LALLY

Dumbledore has a brother?

64 INT. HOG'S HEAD—LATER—NIGHT

Aberforth offers the Qilin a saucer of milk. Instantly, the Qilin perks up, making all manner of happy sounds as it leans over and slurps. Bunty looks on.

Just then, the front door RATTLES and the rush of wind and scatterings of snow sail into the pub. The sound of VOICES and the STAMPING OF BOOTS precedes the entrance of Dumbledore, Newt, Theseus, Lally, and Jacob.

NEWT

Bunty! You're here!

BUNTY

Yes.

NEWT

How is she?

BUNTY

Oh, she's fine.

Newt bends down as a Niffler runs toward him.

NEWT

Whoa, what's Alfie done now? You've
not been biting Timothy's bottom again,
have you?

DUMBLEDORE

Miss Broadacre. I trust my brother has
been a gracious host?

BUNTY

Yes. Ever so gracious.

Dumbledore glances at his brother.

DUMBLEDORE

I'm delighted to hear. So, rooms have
been arranged for you in the village,
and Aberforth here will prepare you a
delicious dinner. His own recipe.

We CUT TO:

65 INT. HOG'S HEAD—LATER—NIGHT

*PLOP! Aberforth, greasy pot in hand, LADLES a thick grayish
STEW into the chipped bowls sitting before the group, who sit
at a long table.*

ABERFORTH
There's more of that if you want it.

The others stare queasily at their bowls as Aberforth heads for the stairs.

BUNTY
Thank you. Thanks.

Aberforth pauses, glowering down at a smiling Bunty, then nods shortly and continues on up.

THESEUS
Astonishing . . . Never has something
that looked so repellent tasted so
delicious.

The Qilin BLEATS with pleasure. The others all dip their spoons.

JACOB
Who's this little one . . . Hey, do you
mind?

Newt watches Jacob jockeying with the Qilin over the stew in his bowl.

NEWT

She's a Qilin, Jacob. She's incredibly rare.
One of the most beloved creatures in the
wizarding world.

JACOB

Why?

NEWT

Because she can see into your soul.

JACOB

Oh, you're kidding me.

NEWT

(shaking his head)

So if you're good and worthy, then she'll
see that. If, on the other hand, you're
cruel and deceitful, then she will know
that too.

JACOB

Oh yeah? Does she just tell you that
or . . . ?

NEWT

Not exactly *tells*—

LALLY

Well, she bows. But only in the presence
of someone truly pure of heart.

Jacob gazes at Lally, captivated.

LALLY (CONT'D)

I mean, almost none of us are, of course.
No matter how good a person we try to be.
There was actually a time, many, many
years ago, when the Qilin chose who
would lead us.

Jacob takes his bowl and moves to the Qilin's milk bowl. The Qilin dances around him. Jacob spoons some of the stew into the Qilin's bowl.

Newt smiles, enjoying the moment, when his gaze catches sight of the mirror. Words are surfacing, one by one:

I WANT TO COME HOME.

66 INT. UPPER ROOM—HOG'S HEAD—MOMENTS LATER—NIGHT

Within, Dumbledore and Aberforth stand opposite each other, their voices low, but their postures suggesting their discussion is tense.

DUMBLEDORE
Come with me. I'll help you. He's your
son, Aberforth. He needs you.

*We see the POV is Newt's. He begins to turn away when he
notices something in Aberforth's hand: a FEATHER, strewn
with ASH, darkening Aberforth's fingers where he touches it.
A PHOENIX FEATHER.*

Newt knocks . . .

DUMBLEDORE (CONT'D)
Newt.

*Aberforth brushes past Newt wordlessly, still clutching
the feather.*

DUMBLEDORE (CONT'D)
(to Newt)
Come in.

Newt enters.

NEWT
Albus. The mirror downstairs. There's a
message.

FANTASTIC BEASTS

DUMBLEDORE

Close the door.

Newt closes the door, then turns back to Dumbledore.

DUMBLEDORE (CONT'D)

It's from Credence, Newt. The summer
Gellert and I fell in love, my brother
fell in love as well. With a girl from the
Hollow. She was sent away. There were
rumors. About a child.

NEWT

Credence?

DUMBLEDORE

He's a Dumbledore. Had I been a better
friend, to Aberforth . . . If I'd been a
better brother, he might have confided
in me. Perhaps things would have been
different. This boy could have been part
of our lives. Part of our family.

(a beat)

Credence can't be saved, I know you
know that. But he may yet be able to
save *us*.

As Newt reacts, Dumbledore holds up his hand, fingers stained with soot.

> DUMBLEDORE (CONT'D)
> Phoenix ash. The bird comes to him
> because he's dying, Newt. I know the signs.
> *(off Newt's look)*
> You see, my sister was an Obscurial.

Newt stares at Dumbledore. Stunned.

> DUMBLEDORE (CONT'D)
> And like Credence, she never learned
> to express her magic. Over time it grew
> darker and began to poison her.

Dumbledore looks to the painting.

> DUMBLEDORE (CONT'D)
> Worst of all, none of us were capable of
> easing her pain.

> NEWT
> Can you tell me how it is—how it came
> to an end for her?

THE
DUMBLEDORE
FAMILY
TREE

The Dumbledores originally lived in Mould-on-the-Wold, but moved to Godric's Hollow after Percival Dumbledore was sent to Azkaban for attacking Muggles; he did not inform the authorities that his actions were in retaliation for the Muggles' traumatising attack on his daughter, Ariana. The Dumbledores were the subject of much gossip, since Ariana was rarely seen, and a fist fight broke out at her funeral between her older brothers.

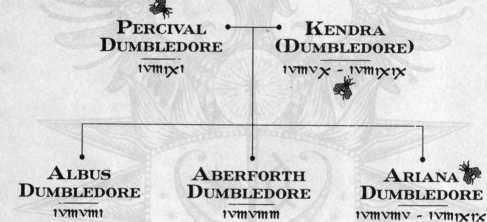

PERCIVAL
DUMBLEDORE
ɪᴠᴍɪxɪ

KENDRA
(DUMBLEDORE)
ɪᴠᴍᴠx - ɪᴠᴍɪxɪx

ALBUS
DUMBLEDORE
ɪᴠᴍᴠɪɪɪ

ABERFORTH
DUMBLEDORE
ɪᴠᴍᴠɪɪɪ

ARIANA
DUMBLEDORE
ɪᴠᴍᴠɪɪᴠ - ɪᴠᴍɪxɪx

he Dumbledores Nullam lobortis ullamcorper purus eget semper purus dignissim quis. Proin et tortor nisl. Sed nec massa volutpat diam tempus hendrerit. Donec vitae nisl ligula. Curabitur sit amet lacus lacinia. ultricies enim quis ornare nisl. Ut nec tincidunt ipsum, vel ultricies tortor. Sed feugiat consectetur ultrices. Aenean nibh massa, ultricies id odio sit amet placerat tristique est. Cras tincidunt sit amet nibh sit amet consequat. Pellentesque sollicitudin dignissim lacus sed sagittis est molestie vel. Sed sodales convallis neque, vitae molestie mi feugiat venenatis. Ut id aliquet erat a aliquet tortor.

Mauris accumsan, ligula sit amet eleifend suscipit diam lacus tempus enim, nec luctus dolor velit sit amet lacus. Sed in pellentesque dui. Praesent lacus tellus semper non lacus at dictum condimentum massa. The Dumbledores venenatis sem a bibendum eleifend lacus metus commodo erat ut con-

consequat odio lorem nec nisl. Proin vitae volutpat felis. Nulla et dolor consequat erat iaculis viverra vel sit amet tortor. Nam metus justo semper sed consectetur at convallis at. The Dumbledores mi. Duis in odio sagittis vestibulum odio ut ullamcorper ante. Nullam in rutrum risus et ullamcorper quam. Vestibulum sit amet egestas elit a mattis quam.

The Dumbledores vehicula elementum. Donec feugiat justo a: tempor scelerisque. Proin tincidunt et ipsum non lacinia. Suspendisse venenatis libero quis efficitur placerat velit ipsum convallis velit, quis egestas felis erat eu justo. The Dumbledores Vestibulum at finibus nunc. Nam sed facilisis dui, vel dictum ipsum. Curabitur nec fermentum sapien. Phasellus tortor. The Dumbledores leo facilisis quis eros in, interdum placerat tortor. Duis in odio sagittis vestibulum odio ut ullamcorper ante. Nullam in rutrum risus et ullamcorper quam ed facilisis dui.

(above) **DUMBLEDORE FAMILY CREST**

(opposite) **PRELIMINARY GRAPHIC FOR DUMBLEDORE FAMILY TREE**

DUMBLEDORE

Gellert and I had made plans to go away together. My brother didn't approve. One night, he confronted us. Voices were raised. Threats made. Aberforth drew his wand, which was foolish. I drew my wand, which was even more foolish. Gellert just laughed. No one heard Ariana coming down the stairs.

Dumbledore's eyes glitter as he stares at the painting.

DUMBLEDORE (CONT'D)

I can't say for certain it was my spell. It doesn't really matter. One minute she was there, and the next she was gone . . .

His voice trails off.

NEWT

I'm so sorry, Albus. If it's of any comfort, perhaps she was saved some pain—

DUMBLEDORE

Don't. Don't disappoint me, Newt. You of all people. Your honesty is a gift, even if at times a painful one.

Newt studies Dumbledore as he stares off toward the painting once more.

> DUMBLEDORE (CONT'D)
> Our friends downstairs will be tired and
> wanting to go home. You should go.

Newt begins to exit, then stops just shy of the door.

> NEWT
> Albus. Lally said something earlier.
> About most of us ultimately being
> imperfect. But even if we've made
> mistakes, terrible things, we can try
> to make things right. And that's what
> matters. The trying.

Dumbledore doesn't turn, just stares at the painting.

67 EXT. NURMENGARD CASTLE—LATE DAY

The camera circles high across the slate sky above the castle. Far below, we see an ARMY OF DARK-CLAD FIGURES assembled. As Grindelwald and Credence make their way toward the castle, the figures part. Reaching the entrance, Grindelwald turns, surveying them.

GRINDELWALD
Our time is close, my brothers and
sisters. The days of hiding are over. The
world will hear our voice. And it will be
deafening.

A ROAR goes up amongst the throng. Grindelwald smiles faintly, then his eyes fix on Kama, standing to one side in front of the cheering Acolytes, somehow both a part of the throng and separate. Grindelwald steps over to him and, to Kama's surprise, takes his face in both hands.

GRINDELWALD (CONT'D)
You didn't come here to betray
Dumbledore. You know in your pure-
blood heart your place is here. To believe
in me is to believe in yourself.

He stares deeply into Kama's eyes one more moment and walks him down into the crowd, gently pushing him into the assembled troops.

GRINDELWALD (CONT'D)
Prove your loyalty, Mr. Kama.

Then releases him, before turning for the castle.

HISTORICALLY, wizards and witches have not been treated well by people. And—just to give my own take on his backstory—I have a hunch that Grindelwald experienced something unforgivable or even extremely brutal at a very young age, and that was when his hatred of Muggles began. It just grew stronger and stronger and every passing day confirmed his belief that there's nothing good in Muggles.

—MADS MIKKELSEN
(Gellert Grindelwald)

68 INT. CELLAR—NURMENGARD—MOMENTS LATER—LATE DAY

CLOSE ON—THE DEAD QILIN.

As the limp creature's head flops to one side, the laceration across its throat is revealed.

. . . UNDERWATER, looking upward through a strangely undulating surface. All is eerily SILENT, like a dream, then a FIGURE appears—indistinct through the liquid—cradling something. The figure PLUNGES his hands into the water and the face of the DEAD QILIN turns our way. Blood blooms from its ragged throat.

NEW ANGLE—GRINDELWALD

He stands waist-deep in a pool, shirtsleeves rolled up past his elbows, holding the Qilin underwater as he murmurs indistinctly. He waits for the water to grow still, then WHISPERS:

> **GRINDELWALD**
> *Rennervate . . .*

Credence, Vogel, and Rosier watch from the shadows.

With great tenderness, Grindelwald plays his fingers over the Qilin's throat, mending the flesh there. BUBBLES rise from the

pool. The Qilin's head breaks the surface and it SCREECHES. Grindelwald lifts it from the water.

GRINDELWALD (CONT'D)
Vulnera Sanentur . . .

As the scars vanish under his fingertips, the Qilin turns its head to him, its eyes still eerily vacant, but otherwise appearing healthy and whole.

Grindelwald smiles, strokes it.

GRINDELWALD (CONT'D)
There, there. There, there . . .
(*without turning*)
Come look.

Vogel glances away, staying put, but Credence leaves the shadows and goes to the edge of the pool.

GRINDELWALD
This is why we're special. To conceal
our powers is not merely an affront to
ourselves. It's sinful.

Grindelwald places the Qilin at the side of the pool, where it stays standing. Credence studies the newly reborn Qilin, bewitched. Gratified by Credence's reaction, Grindelwald looks

back to the Qilin . . . then stops, his smile faltering. A PALE SHADOW, identical to the Qilin in his hands, appears briefly within the currents of the water. His eyes harden.

> GRINDELWALD (CONT'D)
> Was there another?

> CREDENCE
> Another?

> GRINDELWALD
> That night. Was there another Qilin?

In the shadows, Vogel turns, looks back to the pool. Grindelwald's eyes are pinched with fury. Credence, his face pale and slick, looks suddenly uneasy.

> CREDENCE
> I don't think so—

With frightening speed, Grindelwald throws Credence back from the pool with a powerful burst of water and pins him to the wall. Grindelwald Apparates from the water, his fingers laced about Credence's throat and face. His eyes glitter with anger.

> GRINDELWALD
> That's twice you've failed me! Do you not
> understand the danger you've put me in?!

Credence remains frozen like a terrified child under Grindelwald's grip.

GRINDELWALD (CONT'D)

One last chance. Understood? Find it.

69 INT. HOG'S HEAD—MORNING

Newt is inside his case.

Theseus is holding the Qilin, like a baby.

Theseus hands the Qilin to Newt, the pair like two doting parents. Theseus and Bunty look on as Newt gently lowers the Qilin into his case.

70 EXT. HOGWARTS—SAME TIME—MORNING

Mist hangs over the grounds. Bridge and castle glow softly in the morning light.

71 INT. 7TH FLOOR CORRIDOR—HOGWARTS—SAME TIME—MORNING

We follow Lally, Newt, Theseus, and Jacob toward an ornate door emerging from the wall at the far end of the corridor.

HOGWARTS EXTERIOR LOCATION RENDERING

72 INT. ROOM OF REQUIREMENT—MOMENTS LATER—MORNING

Newt, Theseus, Lally, and Jacob suddenly appear in a sparsely appointed room.

Jacob, looking utterly confused, follows Newt's gaze to the far end of the room, where FIVE CASES—identical to Newt's— stand in a circle in front of a huge, ornate BHUTANESE PRAYER WHEEL. Bunty stands by the cases.

> JACOB
> Hey, Newt, what is this place?

> NEWT
> The room we require.

Dumbledore strides into view.

> DUMBLEDORE
> I trust all of you have the tickets that
> Bunty gave you?

Nods all around. Jacob dutifully holds his up for all to see.

> DUMBLEDORE (CONT'D)
> You'll need them to gain access to the
> ceremony.

"THE WALK OF THE QILIN" TICKET DESIGN

Dumbledore's eyes shift, clock Newt staring at the circle of cases.

> DUMBLEDORE (CONT'D)
> What do you think, Newt? Can you tell which one is yours?

Newt looks another moment, then shakes his head.

> NEWT
> No.

> DUMBLEDORE
> Good. I'd be worried if you could.

> LALLY
> I assume the Qilin's in one of these cases?

> DUMBLEDORE
> Yes.

> LALLY
> Well, which one is it?

> DUMBLEDORE
> Which one indeed.

JACOB

Oh, it's like a three-card monte thing.
(as the others eye him)
Like a shell game thing. Like a short con.
(giving up)
Never mind, it's a Muggle thing.

DUMBLEDORE

Grindelwald will do anything within
his power to get his hands on our
rare friend. Therefore it's essential we
keep whoever he dispatches on his
behalf guessing so the Qilin gets to
the ceremony safely. If by teatime, the
Qilin—not to mention all of us—are
still alive, we should consider our efforts
a success.

Dumbledore puts his hat on and wraps a scarf around his neck.

JACOB

For the record, no one ever died playing
three-card monte.

DUMBLEDORE

An important distinction. All right,
everyone choose a case and we'll be on

NEWT'S CASE AND REPLICAS

our way. Mr. Kowalski, you and I will
proceed together first.

JACOB

Me? Okay . . .

*Jacob steps forward, selects a case, then stops as Dumble-
dore clears his throat and almost imperceptibly shakes his
head. Jacob selects another and points. Dumbledore nods and
turns away.*

Jacob picks up the case. Nods. Glances around. Frowns. No exit.

*The Bhutanese prayer wheel glitters in front of Dumbledore.
He reaches out, touches it, and a beautiful glow fills the room.*

DUMBLEDORE (CONT'D)

I'm looking forward to you educating
me a little further on the finer points of
three-card monte.

He looks over to Jacob, reaches out his hand to him.

JACOB

My pleasure.

*Jacob takes Dumbledore's hand, and together they disappear
into the wheel as it rapidly spins.*

As they vanish, the others consider the remaining cases.

BUNTY

Well, good luck, everybody.

Newt walks forward and picks up a case.

NEWT

Good luck.

Newt vanishes.

LALLY

And you too, Bunty girl.

Lally walks forward, picks up another case, and vanishes.

THESEUS

See you, Bunty.

Theseus walks forward and picks up another case before disappearing into the wheel too.

Bunty takes a deep breath, then picks up the last case. She walks toward the prayer wheel and vanishes.

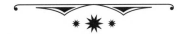
73 EXT. BASE OF EYRIE—BHUTAN—DAY

Green mountains rise in the distance, and at the very top, almost settled into the very sky, we glimpse the Eyrie.

A crowd gathers at the base of an enormous set of steps that climb toward the sky, on top of which sits the magnificent Eyrie. A figure stands in front of a gilded cage set beneath the steps.

> VOGEL
>
> It is not lost on those of us in leadership that we are currently a world divided. Each day brings talk of another conspiracy.

Vogel's speech is seen projected into Magical Ministries around the world.

> VOGEL (CONT'D)
>
> Each hour another dark whisper. These whispers have only increased in recent days with the addition of a third candidate. There is only one way to leave absolutely no doubt that a worthy candidate exists amongst the three who have been presented.

EYRIE LOCATION RENDERING

THE WALK OF THE QILIN

Vogel enters the golden cage and emerges with something cradled in his arms. As he resumes his place and slowly reveals what he holds, there is a palpable GASP.

A Qilin.

> VOGEL (CONT'D)
> As every schoolboy and girl knows: The Qilin is the purest of creatures in our wonderful, magical world. It cannot be deceived.
> *(holding it before him)*
> Let the Qilin unite us!

74 EXT. ROOFTOPS—BHUTAN—DAY

We drop through layers of cloud to a village and a series of terraced rooftops, where dark-clad figures appear. Rosier stands at the head of one group, Helmut the other. They scan the streets below, at the massing crowds, eyes searching.

75 EXT. STREET—BHUTAN—SAME TIME—DAY

Bobbing along with a group of Santos supporters, case in hand, is Jacob and next to him, keeping point, Dumbledore. Just ahead of them, a vast BANNER bearing Santos's image twists on the poles carrying it as the supporters march toward the mountains beyond the city.

Just then, Dumbledore's gaze lands on a group of Dark Aurors trailing close behind and he pulls Jacob ducking and swerving into an alley. They Apparate out of a doorway behind their pursuers and give them the slip.

DUMBLEDORE

Come.

JACOB

Where to next?

DUMBLEDORE

Oh. This is where I leave you.

JACOB

I'm sorry, you're what? You're leaving me?

Dumbledore takes off his scarf.

DUMBLEDORE

I have to meet someone else, Mr. Kowalski.
Not to worry. You'll be perfectly safe.

Dumbledore casts off his scarf. As it flutters through the air, the scarf morphs into a curtain. Dumbledore turns back to Jacob.

BHUTAN LOCATION RENDERING

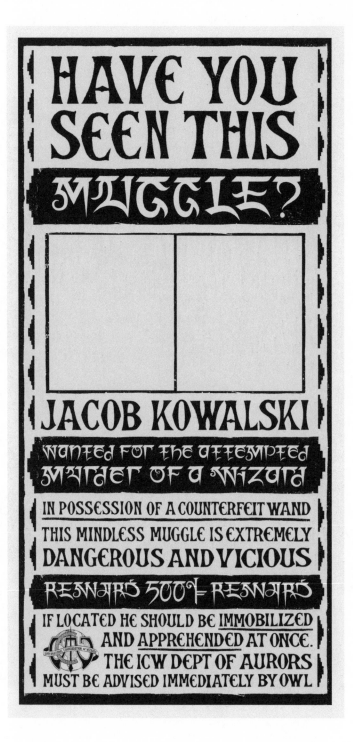

PRELIMINARY GRAPHIC FOR WANTED POSTER, WITH SPACE LEFT
FOR MOVING PHOTOGRAPHS OF JACOB KOWALSKI

> DUMBLEDORE (CONT'D)
> You don't have the Qilin. Feel free to
> drop the case at the first hint of trouble.
> *(stopping)*
> One other thing, if you don't mind
> me saying. You should stop doubting
> yourself. You have something most men
> go their entire lives without. Do you
> know what that is?

Jacob shakes his head.

> DUMBLEDORE (CONT'D)
> A heart that is full. Only a truly brave
> man could open himself up so honestly
> and completely. As you do.

With that, Dumbledore tips his hat and is gone.

76 EXT. STREET—BHUTAN—SAME TIME—DAY

*Newt moves quickly, trying his best to remain inconspicuous.
Sensing something, he stops. Turns.*

No one.

BHUTAN LOCATION RENDERING

77   EXT. NARROW STREET—BHUTAN—SAME TIME—DAY

Theseus moves warily forward, case held tightly.

78   EXT. NARROW STREET—BHUTAN—SAME TIME—DAY

Newt proceeds through the village. A GREEN-ROBED FIGURE comes into frame.

79   EXT. STREET—BHUTAN—SAME TIME—DAY

We follow a case, Lally, moving quickly. Glimpsing ahead, she sees Aurors. She turns into an alley and disappears from view.

80   EXT. STREET—BHUTAN—SAME TIME—DAY

Theseus moves warily through a narrow passage. We see figures shifting on the rooftops above him. Ahead, he spots two Aurors and draws his wand.

81   EXT. BACK STREETS—BHUTAN—SAME TIME—DAY

Lally moves quickly, glancing over her shoulder when . . .

82 EXT. JUNCTION—BACK STREETS—BHUTAN—SAME TIME—DAY

. . . she comes together with Theseus at the junction of their respective streets. Both whirl, raise their wands . . . then recognize each other. Then, as one, their gazes shift. Around them, everywhere, are DARK AURORS.

Lally and Theseus deflect, parry, and duel the Dark Aurors from all sides, retreating up the steps as they fire a flurry of counter spells and charms.

Lally Stuns three Dark Aurors, Theseus Stuns half a dozen more. Lally levitates a dozen crystal balls and sends them cascading toward the Aurors as Theseus Stuns a Dark Auror on a balcony above them. Turning, Lally incapacitates another by wrapping him in fabric before sending an Auror shooting into a wall and imprisoning him there as if stuck in a portrait.

Aurors are left sprawled all over the street before them. Their victory is short-lived, though, as two wands appear, drawn at the backs of their necks . . .

HELMUT

Cases, please.

Helmut stands behind them, flanked by two Dark Aurors.

BHUTAN LOCATION RENDERING

83   EXT. ALLEYS/STONE STEPS—BHUTAN—SAME TIME—DAY

Newt rounds a corner, and in the distance he sees two Aurors emerge ahead.

Just beyond, he spots someone else.

> JACOB
> Hey, fellas . . .

The Aurors turn, and TWHACK, Jacob sends both spinning with a swing of his case before darting out of sight. The Aurors recover and give chase.

84   EXT. NARROW ALLEY, LEADING UPWARD—SAME TIME—DAY

Jacob stumbles around a corner and races up some steep, narrow steps. Moments later, his pursuers come into view, stop, and stare upward.

Empty.

Except for Jacob's case.

85   EXT. BACK STREETS—BHUTAN—SAME TIME—DAY

Helmut and his men take Lally's and Theseus's cases and set them down. A Dark Auror takes aim. Helmut raises his hand.

HELMUT

Wait. Open them. Make sure it's in
there. Idiot.

The Auror trapped in the wall bangs with his fists to be let out. With a sigh, Helmut raises his wand and releases him, sending him sprawling to the ground with a thud.

Lally and Theseus glance at the cases.

86 EXT. BACK STREETS—BHUTAN—SAME TIME—DAY

One of Jacob's pursuers tentatively approaches the abandoned case.

As Lally and Theseus look on, two of Helmut's Dark Aurors kneel beside the cases.

POP! Jacob's case flips open to REVEAL . . . POLISH PASTRIES.

Lally's and Theseus's cases are opened, revealing BOOKS and the GOLDEN SNITCH.

The Dark Auror hovering over Jacob's case grabs a paczki and inspects it.

As the Golden Snitch BUZZES upward, Helmut watches it rise past the surrounding rooftops when:

BHUTAN LOCATION RENDERING

WHOOSH!

The books erupt out of Lally's case and engulf the Dark Aurors, mummifying them in a windstorm of paper.

Jacob's case erupts with thousands of pastries cascading in a wave that sweeps the Dark Aurors down the steep steps and away.

The Monster Book of Monsters *attacks as Bludgers fly out of Theseus's case and catapult into the Dark Aurors in the alley and atop the rooftops high above.*

Helmut furiously strips a piece of paper from his face only to discover, in the chaos, Lally and Theseus have escaped.

87 EXT. STREETS/ALLEYS—BHUTAN—SAME TIME—DAY

Dumbledore moves swiftly, glancing to a nearby rooftop as Bludgers rain down upon the Aurors and send them tumbling. A Snitch buzzes down toward him, and he catches it midair and pockets it. Suddenly, in lockstep, from an alleyway, a figure joins him.

Never breaking stride, Aberforth.

> **ABERFORTH**
> How long does he have?

THE PHOENIX FLIES OVERHEAD . . .

88 EXT. STREET—BHUTAN—DAY

. . . skating over the mass of people streaming far below.

NEW ANGLE—STREET LEVEL

Credence, looking ever more pale, bumps along amidst the jubilant throng of Liu supporters. Weakened and in pain, he pauses, leaning against a pillar before steeling himself once more and moving on.

89 EXT. NARROW ALLEY LEADING UPWARD—BHUTAN—DAY

Jacob, case-less now, walks down a narrow alley. He feeds onto a street. He passes a GREEN-ROBED FIGURE when another figure sweeps in and grabs him firmly by the hand . . .

. . . pulling him into a side street and away from the main street.

> QUEENIE
> You're in danger, all right. You need to
> leave.

> JACOB
> Well . . .

CREDENCE yearns, like so many of Jo's characters, to belong. And he feels in his heart that he cannot count on Grindelwald. He's also very sick—the Obscurus seems to be taking him over more and more. So as he faces his own mortality, he is trying to figure out just where he belongs at this point in his life.

—DAVID HEYMAN
(Producer)

As he starts to speak, she puts a finger over his lips.

QUEENIE

I can't. I can't come home. It's too late
for me. Some mistakes are just too big.

Jacob takes her hand away.

JACOB

Can you listen to me—

QUEENIE

There's no time! I was followed. I gave
them the slip, but it won't be long before
they find me.
They're going to find . . .
(*voice breaking*)
. . . us.

JACOB

I don't care. All I got is us. I make no
sense without us.

QUEENIE

Jacob, come on! I don't love you
anymore. Just get out of here.

        JACOB
You're the worst liar in the world,
Queenie Goldstein.

Just then, CHURCH BELLS peal softly.

        JACOB (CONT'D)
You hear that? That's a sign.

She stops, glaring at him. He stares at her.

Jacob enfolds Queenie's hand in his and pulls her close.

        JACOB (CONT'D)
Come here. Close your eyes. Please close
your eyes. You know what Dumbledore
said to me? He said that I got a full
heart . . . He's wrong, I'm always going
to have room in there for you.

        QUEENIE
Yeah.

        JACOB
Look at me. Queenie Goldstein . . .

As a tear trickles down her cheek, they both look up to see FIGURES surrounding them.

90   EXT. BRIDGE—BHUTAN—SAME TIME—DAY

Newt watches as Santos supporters cross a BRIDGE that rises into the sky; they disappear through a portal partway across. He grips his case tighter and moves forward, mingling with the crowd.

From this vantage, the mountain looms mightily, its peak draped in thick clouds.

Newt makes his way onto the bridge, toward the portal. Stepping through it, he disappears with a whoosh.

91   EXT. BASE OF EYRIE—BHUTAN—DAY

At the base of the Eyrie we see vast steps rising up to the clouds and the Eyrie above. We drop down to reveal Newt, striding purposefully, in the direction of the steps.

Directly ahead, a solitary figure, Fischer, stands unmoving. She turns, eyes focused on Newt. There is something ominous in her posture.

Newt, debating a detour, but there is only one way up when . . .

EYRIE LOCATION RENDERING

BHUTAN LOCATION RENDERING

FISCHER

Mr. Scamander. We've never been
properly introduced. Henrietta Fischer.
Herr Vogel's attaché.

NEWT

Ah, yes— Hello—

She nods to the clouds overhead.

FISCHER

I can take you up. There's a private
entrance for members of the High
Council. If you just follow me . . .

Newt doesn't move, eyeing her skeptically.

NEWT

I'm sorry, why would you do that? Take
me up?

FISCHER

Isn't it obvious?

NEWT

No, frankly, it's not.

FISCHER

Dumbledore's sent me.

(the case)

I know what you have in the case, Mr.
Scamander.

As Fischer's eyes narrow, a throng of exuberant Santos, Liu, and Grindelwald supporters spill into view. Quick as a snake, Fischer's hand snatches Newt's where he grips the handle. They lock eyes, and Newt makes to wrest the case free while the crowd converges. They continue to wrestle over control of the case as they are borne down the middle of the square, surrounded by happy faces and cheering voices.

FLASH!—a bolt of fire strikes Newt behind his ear. He falls. Zabini appears, standing within the crowd, looking down at him, wand SMOKING. Fischer smiles before turning away, carrying the case with her.

92 EXT. BRIDGE—BHUTAN—SAME TIME

Theseus paces nervously as Lally stands by. The bridge is nearly deserted now. A HORN, like a CLARION CALL, rises over the city.

LALLY

He should be here any minute.

Just ahead, Kama and a group of Dark Aurors appear, heading toward them. The Dark Aurors raise their wands. Kama moves through the Aurors.

Kama suddenly drops, driving his wand into the earth, releasing a pulse of magic that stuns the Aurors, concussing them instantly.

> THESEUS
> What kept you?

Theseus, Lally, and Kama head onto the bridge and disappear.

93   EXT. BASE OF EYRIE—BHUTAN—DAY

Coming to, Newt glances about frantically, buffeted by the crowd . . .

He sees Fischer making her way up the stairs ahead.

Towering above supporters and voters are massive freestanding BANNERS, which act as SCREENS to reflect the ceremony above. As Newt stares at the banner—in reflection—Vogel appears.

> VOGEL
> I thank the candidates for their words . . .

94 EXT. EYRIE—BHUTAN—CONTINUOUS—DAY

Liu, Santos, and Grindelwald stand side by side.

> VOGEL
> Each represents a distinct vision of how
> we will shape not only our world, but
> the non-magical world as well. Which
> brings us to the most important part of
> our ceremony. The walk of the Qilin.

A Qilin is brought forth.

We CUT TO:

95 EXT. EYRIE—BHUTAN—SAME TIME—DAY

*Newt reaches the great steps that stretch up to the Eyrie, seeing
a tiny figure up ahead with his case—Fischer.*

*As he pounds up the steps, he looks across to the banners and
sees the Qilin being put before Grindelwald, Liu, and Santos.*

*A QUICK TOUR AROUND THE WORLD, as dignitaries at
MAGICAL MINISTRIES, in EUROPE and elsewhere, watch
the ceremony.*

On the screen the Qilin moves tentatively forward—toward the candidates. As the Qilin moves toward Grindelwald, Liu and Santos exchange a glance.

Newt charges toward Fischer, who simply turns to look at Newt, making no effort to move.

The Qilin stands in front of Grindelwald and gazes up at him.

Fischer holds out the case. Newt studies her, perplexed by her demeanor, then reaches out. As his fingers make contact, the case turns to dust. In a panic, he watches the particles drift into the air. He looks back to Fischer, who continues to smile.

As the dust drifts up, the banners reveal Grindelwald and the Qilin.

The Qilin, in front of Grindelwald, bows. For a moment, there is a long beat of silence.

> VOGEL
> The Qilin has seen. Seen goodness,
> strength, qualities essential to lead, and
> to guide us. Who do you see?

The assembled witches and wizards thrust their wands into the air. SPELLS explode. The THREE COLORS of Liu, Santos, and Grindelwald stream into the sky and then turn to one, Grindelwald's green.

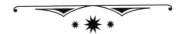

Newt stands stunned.

Grindelwald savors the adulation.

> VOGEL (CONT'D)
> Gellert Grindelwald is the new leader of
> the magical world by acclamation.

As the crowd ROARS, Acolytes on either side of Newt shove him up the steps. Grindelwald nods to Rosier and she brings forth Queenie and Jacob.

Newt tries to push his way toward Queenie and Jacob, but the two Acolytes restrain him.

Rosier brings Jacob farther up the steps and hands his snake-wood wand to Grindelwald.

Grindelwald surveys the crowd, who waits, eyes fixed on him, then gestures to Jacob.

> GRINDELWALD
> This is the man who tried to take my life.
> This man who has no magic, who would
> marry a witch and pollute our blood.
> This forbidden union will make us less,
> make us weak, like his kind. He is not
> alone, my friends. There are thousands

who seek to do the same. There can only
be one response to such *vermin*.

Grindelwald tosses away Jacob's wand and raises his own.

As Jacob turns to face him, Grindelwald hits him with a spell that throws him down the steps and sends him sprawling onto his back at Queenie's feet.

GRINDELWALD (CONT'D)
Crucio!

A lightning spell sends Jacob writhing in pain at Queenie's feet.

NEWT
No!

QUEENIE
Make him stop!

GRINDELWALD
Our war with the Muggles begins today!

Grindelwald's SUPPORTERS CHEER wildly.

Lally, Theseus, and Kama can be seen moving through the crowd, looking shocked.

Jacob remains writhing in pain on the ground until Santos raises her wand and lifts the Cruciatus Curse afflicting him. Relieved, Jacob lies back in Queenie's arms.

Grindelwald turns his face to the sky, basking in his glory.

He stays like this, reveling in the moment when . . .

. . . he spies the Phoenix circling overhead. A solitary feather of ASH seesaws from the sky and attaches itself to his cheek. He wipes it away, looking troubled.

Grindelwald turns, squinting, as a FIGURE emerges from the steps . . .

Credence.

Grindelwald studies him with interest as he approaches, looking weak but defiant. As he stops in front of Grindelwald, he reaches out, as if he were going to cradle Grindelwald's face, then takes his fingers and smears the ash on his cheek. Aberforth and Dumbledore emerge at the back of the crowd as Credence turns, addressing the dignitaries.

CREDENCE

He's lying to you. That creature is dead.

Newt regards the bewitched Qilin sadly.

Nearing the end of his strength, Credence falls to his knees.

Aberforth moves to help him, but is held back gently by Dumbledore.

>   DUMBLEDORE
> Not now. Wait.

Newt pulls free of his captors.

>   NEWT
> He did it to trick you. He killed it and
> bewitched it so that you might think
> him worthy to lead. But he doesn't want
> to lead you, he just wants you to follow.

>   GRINDELWALD
> Words. Words designed to deceive. To
> make you doubt what you've seen with
> your own two eyes.

>   NEWT
> There were two Qilins born that night. A
> twin. And I know that, I know that—

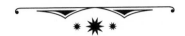
GRINDELWALD

Because . . . ? Because you have no proof.
Because there was no second Qilin. Am I
not right?

NEWT

Its mother had been killed.

GRINDELWALD

Then where is it now, Mr. Scamander?

*Grindelwald looks at Newt, triumphant, when his gaze falls to
a green-robed dignitary . . .*

*She steps forward, into the light, a CASE in hand, and gives it
to Newt, who stares at it, dumbfounded.*

The robed figure looks up to reveal . . . Bunty.

BUNTY

No one can know everything, Newt.
Remember?

*She glances around, abruptly—and uncomfortably—aware of
the dignified persons present, then moves away as Newt opens
the lid of the case.*

A small head emerges, looks about.

The Qilin.

Vogel stares incredulously, nervously eyeing Grindelwald, who looks unsettled as well. Theseus and Lally exchange stunned glances. Tina watches on from the AMERICAN MINISTRY. Newt, more stunned than anyone, smiles—looking relieved, grateful.

As everyone watches, the Qilin crawls out of the case and stands upright, blinking in confusion, trying to get its bearings. Then, sensing something, it turns and sees:

The bewitched Qilin, standing by Grindelwald's side.

Instantly, the Qilin SOFTLY KEENS, calling out, the sound heartbreaking in its naked emotion, but its twin's expression remains unchanged, its eyes blank.

Newt kneels down beside the confused Qilin.

NEWT
(softly)

She can't hear you, little one. Not here. But perhaps somewhere she's listening in . . .

VOGEL
This is the true Qilin!

Vogel snatches up the bewitched Qilin and turns to all those watching.

> VOGEL (CONT'D)
> Look at it! You can see it with your own
> eyes . . . This is the true—

He falters as the Qilin in his hands slumps to the side, its eyes dark and empty.

The British Witch we last saw in Berlin steps forward.

> BRITISH WITCH
> This can't be allowed to stand! The vote
> must be taken again. Come on, Anton.
> Do something!

Vogel looks confused, frightened.

The living Qilin is slowly making its way toward Dumbledore.

> DUMBLEDORE
> No. No. No. Please.

The Qilin eyes him carefully, its probing eyes silencing Dumbledore. The Qilin begins to glow and then slowly bows.

Newt looks on curiously, compassionately.

DUMBLEDORE (CONT'D)

I'm honored.

(*a troubled beat*)

Just as two of you were born that night,
there is another here. Equally worthy.
I'm certain of it.

Dumbledore gently strokes the Qilin.

DUMBLEDORE (CONT'D)

Thank you.

*The Qilin eyes Dumbledore curiously before making its way
toward Santos to bow, as Grindelwald watches on with disgust.*

*Grindelwald looks at Dumbledore, consumed by the moment—
and raises his wand toward the Qilin. Credence, seeing Grindelwald taking aim at the Qilin, summons what strength he
has and stands before him.*

*Lightning fast, Grindelwald turns and casts a spell toward
CREDENCE WHEN . . .*

*. . . a BRIGHT, BLINDING SHIELD OF LIGHT materializes in
front of Credence, courtesy of . . .*

*. . . Dumbledore and Aberforth, who—reflexively—indepen-
dently—have cast protective spells.*

As Grindelwald's spell strikes the SHIMMERING SHIELD OF LIGHT, we follow his gaze up the path of the spell and discover . . .

. . . his and Dumbledore's spells have knotted together.

As one, their gazes meet, each stunned to find themselves shackled to the other. For a moment, they remain like this, connected, each draining the power of the other, the world in suspension. Then:

The troth's CHAIN SHATTERS, sending the CRYSTAL slowly spinning to the ground. Grindelwald and Dumbledore watch as the light from the troth begins to FLICKER, and with a FLASH, everything goes suddenly silent . . . The world goes slowly STILL, as if the rotation of the earth itself were slowing.

The troth continues to spin slowly through the air, its center cracking.

Their spells evaporate. Grindelwald's and Dumbledore's eyes meet, both realizing in the same moment that they have been emancipated.

Instantly, their wands rise, FLASHING again and again—fire and parry, fire and parry—in a dizzying—and cathartic— display of power. As they continue to battle, they draw closer and closer, neither able to get the best of the other, neither

willing to concede, until finally, nearly face-to-face, their arms cross and they . . .

Stop. Chests heaving. Eyes locked on each other. Dumbledore reaches out, delicately puts his hand on Grindelwald's heart. Grindelwald does the same, hand on Dumbledore's.

Dumbledore, head bowed, peers up into Grindelwald's eyes.

Just then, a THIN THREAD of YELLOW LIGHT stitches its way up into the sky from the crowd below. Moments later, another THREAD of YELLOW LIGHT joins it. Then another.

Grindelwald watches, his face betraying an impending dread.

Dumbledore watches more threads of light knit their way into the sky and, looking strangely moved, turns away, making to rejoin the frozen world behind him.

Grindelwald stands stricken.

GRINDELWALD
Who will love you now, Dumbledore?

The blood troth strikes the floor.

CRACK.

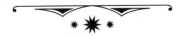

It breaks in two, and smoke rises from its center . . . The world begins to rotate on its axis once more, the figures surrounding Grindelwald and Dumbledore coming back to life.

Dumbledore doesn't turn, leaving Grindelwald behind, to stand alone.

GRINDELWALD (CONT'D)
You're all alone.

Instantly, a THOUSAND YELLOW THREADS LACE THE SKY and all are bathed in a soft yellow light. MAGICAL MINIS-TRIES around the world, including Brazil and France, cheer for Santos, sending their own exploding yellow spells into the air. Grindelwald looks on, defeated.

He gazes over at those who oppose him, unified now as they move toward him, led by Santos and the Qilin, pointing their wands in his direction.

Apparating to the edge, Grindelwald stands backed to the prec-ipice of a great cliff. He rapidly puts a shield around him as spells are cast from those who stand opposite.

But there is only one person who interests him: Dumbledore.

GRINDELWALD (CONT'D)
I was never your enemy. Then or now.

Almost as ONE, spells fly toward Grindelwald, when, with one final glance at Dumbledore . . . he falls backward and Apparates.

Theseus, Lally, and Kama, followed by others, race to the wall edge to see . . .

He's gone.

Dumbledore looks away, sees Aberforth cradling Credence. Credence is weak now, looking at Aberforth curiously, his face bathed in yellow light.

CREDENCE

Did you ever think of me?

ABERFORTH

Always. Come home.

Aberforth reaches his hand out and lifts his son up to his feet. As they begin to descend, Dumbledore watches as the Phoenix takes flight behind them and drifts slowly down the mountain.

Newt looks out over the sea of yellow and the Kingdom of Bhutan beyond. He looks suddenly weary.

BUNTY

Here she is.

WHAT I love about Jo's characters is they are rich; they are never one thing. Grindelwald is very dark, but unlike Voldemort, it's not just that love is absent in his life. I think he feels a deep sadness that Dumbledore—his great love—hasn't joined him on this journey. So, yes, Grindelwald is evil and dark and desirous of power and would stop at nothing to achieve his goals. But beneath that he is filled with a sense of loss, of melancholy.

—DAVID HEYMAN

(Producer)

Newt turns, sees Bunty standing with the Qilin.

> **NEWT**
> Well done, Bunty.

Bunty shakes her head and smiles.

> **NEWT (CONT'D)**
> Come on, little one.

Newt opens the case for the Qilin.

> **BUNTY**
> I'm sorry. I must have given you an
> awful fright.

Newt takes the Qilin. Shakes his head.

> **NEWT**
> No, I think sometimes it takes losing some-
> thing to realize quite how much it means.

Bunty eyes Newt's case as he cradles the Qilin. She spots the picture of Tina and smiles gently.

> **BUNTY**
> And sometimes you just . . .

She falters. Newt studies her.

> BUNTY (CONT'D)
> Sometimes you just know.

She turns away, heading back toward the others.

> NEWT
> In you pop.

As Newt places the Qilin in the case, we CUT TO:

Jacob, watching Dumbledore from a distance.

> DUMBLEDORE
> Mr. Kowalski, I owe you an apology.

Jacob turns, sees Dumbledore.

> DUMBLEDORE (CONT'D)
> It was never my intent for you to suffer
> the Cruciatus Curse.

> JACOB
> Yeah, well, you know, we got Queenie
> back, so we're square.
> *(a beat)*
> Hey, can I ask you a question?

Jacob glances around, then leans forward, WHISPERS.

> ### JACOB (CONT'D)
> Can I keep this? You know, for like old
> times' sake?

Dumbledore looks down, sees the snakewood wand in Jacob's hand, then looks up, studies him.

> ### DUMBLEDORE
> I can't think of anyone more deserving.

> ### JACOB
> Thanks, Professor.

Jacob grins happily and pockets it. Dumbledore watches him head toward Queenie before joining Newt.

Inspecting the edge of the cliff, Dumbledore removes the broken blood troth from his pocket and shows Newt.

> ### DUMBLEDORE
> Remarkable.

> ### NEWT
> But how? I thought you couldn't move
> against one another.

DUMBLEDORE

We didn't. He sought to kill. I sought to
protect. Our spells met.

Dumbledore smiles ruefully.

DUMBLEDORE (CONT'D)

Let's call it fate. After all, how else would
we fulfill our destinies?

Newt eyes him curiously when Theseus joins them.

THESEUS

Albus. Promise me. You'll find him. And
stop him.

Dumbledore nods.

*The yellow sky toward the horizon begins to DISSOLVE, slowly
fading to black . . .*

96 EXT. LOWER EAST SIDE—NEW YORK—NIGHT

*. . . onto a street on the Lower East Side, where the WINDOWS
of KOWALSKI'S BAKERY glow warm with light.*

KOWALSKI BAKERY LOCATION RENDERING

97 INT. KOWALSKI'S BAKERY—CONTINUOUS—NIGHT

PEOPLE flit in and out of view—both Muggle and magical. Jacob's wedding cake now stands proud with the bride and groom on top, reunited.

> JACOB
> Albert! Don't forget the pierogies!

> ALBERT
> Yes, Mr. K.

Jacob and Newt stand in matching MORNING SUITS, Jacob fighting a losing battle with his tie.

> JACOB
> Albert! No more than eight minutes on
> the kolaczkis.

> ALBERT
> Yes, Mr. K.

> JACOB
> *(to Newt)*
> He's a sweet kid. He doesn't know the
> difference between paszteciki and golabki.

Just then, Queenie enters in a BEAUTIFUL LACE GOWN.

QUEENIE

Hey, sweetheart.

JACOB

What!

QUEENIE

Newt doesn't know what you're talking
about. I don't know what you're talking
about. And you are not working today,
remember?
(eyeing Newt)
Are you all right, honey?
(to Newt)
You're nervous about the speech. Don't
be nervous.
(to Jacob)
Tell him, honey—

JACOB

Don't be nervous about the speech.

NEWT

I'm not nervous.

JACOB

What's that smell? Why is there
burning?! Albert!

Jacob rushes off. Queenie rolls her eyes.

> QUEENIE
>
> Maybe we're nervous about something
> else, huh?

> NEWT
>
> I can't imagine what you're talking about.

Queenie smiles knowingly, moves off.

98 EXT. KOWALSKI'S BAKERY—MOMENTS LATER—NIGHT

*Newt steps out under the front awning and takes out a piece of
PAPER. Unfolds it. Begins to MUTTER his speech.*

> NEWT
>
> *The day that I first met Jacob . . . the day
> that I first met Jacob we were both sitting in
> the Steen National Bank . . . Never would I—*

*Newt frowns, looks up. Sees a FIGURE on the bus bench across
the street, sitting in the falling snow.*

*Just then, something tickles the periphery of Newt's vision and
he turns—slowly—to see a WOMAN approaching through the
snow. He doesn't need to look twice. He knows.*

Tina.

NEWT (CONT'D)

The maid of honor, I presume?

TINA

The best man, I gather?

NEWT

You've done something to your hair?

TINA

No. Oh . . . Well, yes, actually, just for tonight.

NEWT

Well, it suits you.

TINA

Thank you, Newt.

They look at each other, no longer talking, when . . .

. . . Lally and Theseus appear.

THESEUS

Hello.

NEWT

Look who's here.

THESEUS

How are you?

NEWT

You look wonderful, Lally.

LALLY

Well, thank you, Newt. I appreciate it.
Good luck.
(to Tina)
Tina. Come on. You must tell me how
MACUSA's been.

They slip inside the bakery.

*Newt goes to follow the others inside, then pauses, looking back
in the direction of the street. A moment passes, then:*

THESEUS

What about me? How do I look? You all
right?

NEWT

You look fine.

THESEUS

You okay?

NEWT

Yeah, I'm all right.

THESEUS

You're not nervous, are you? Can't be
nervous about a speech after saving
the world.

A look between them, and then Newt looks across and sees
Dumbledore sitting on the bus bench opposite.

Newt steps across the snowy street, pauses before the bench.

DUMBLEDORE

It's a historic day. Where once was
before, there will now be after. Funny
how historic days seem so ordinary when
you're living them.

NEWT

Perhaps that's what happens when the
world gets things right.

DUMBLEDORE
It's jolly nice to know it happens
occasionally.

Newt eyes him.

NEWT
I didn't know if I'd see you here.

DUMBLEDORE
I wasn't sure you would either.

Their eyes meet, then Dumbledore looks off. The door to the bakery opens and Queenie appears. Luminous.

QUEENIE
Hey, Newt! Jacob seems to think he's lost
the ring. Please tell me you've got it.

Newt turns and Pickett pops out of his pocket, clutching a SIMPLE BAND with a SMALL, but lovely, CHIP of a DIAMOND.

NEWT
No, it's all good.

She smiles, then disappears inside. Newt looks at Pickett.

NEWT (CONT'D)

Good man, Pick.

(looking at Dumbledore)

I should probably—

Dumbledore says nothing, still staring off.

DUMBLEDORE

Thank you, Newt.

NEWT

What for?

DUMBLEDORE

Pick your poison.

Newt nods.

DUMBLEDORE (CONT'D)

I really couldn't have done it without you.

Newt smiles faintly. Dumbledore merely nods. Newt starts to go, then stops.

NEWT

I'd do it again, by the way. Should you ask.

Newt eyes him curiously, then turns, walks back to the bakery, and disappears inside.

As he closes the door, a YOUNG WOMAN wearing a DRESS PATTERNED IN RED ROSES comes rushing into view.

Looking confused, she glances about in quiet alarm, then spies the bakery.

Bunty.

Dumbledore watches her hurry inside.

He sits another moment, looking around, then rises.

99   INT. KOWALSKI'S BAKERY—CONTINUOUS—NIGHT

Queenie steps forward to join Jacob in front of a MAGICAL MINISTER. Queenie turns and looks at him, as behind, Newt and Tina, Lally, Theseus, Bunty, and Albert gather, watching with emotion.

JACOB

Wow. You're so beautiful.

100 EXT. KOWALSKI'S BAKERY—CONTINUOUS—NIGHT

Dumbledore looks through the window and smiles. He pulls the collar of his coat tight and begins to move off, striding alone through the snow-strewn street toward the wintry horizon in the distance.

LOWER EAST SIDE, NEW YORK, LOCATION RENDERING

J.K. ROWLING is the author of the enduringly popular, era-defining Harry Potter seven-book series, as well as several stand-alone novels for adults and children, and the acclaimed Strike crime fiction series written under the pseudonym Robert Galbraith. Many of her books have been adapted for film and television, and she has collaborated on a play continuing Harry's story onstage, *Harry Potter and the Cursed Child*, and a new series of films inspired by her series companion volume *Fantastic Beasts and Where to Find Them*.

STEVE KLOVES wrote the screenplays for seven of the Harry Potter films, based on the beloved books by J.K. Rowling. He also served as a producer on *Fantastic Beasts and Where to Find Them* and *Fantastic Beasts: The Crimes of Grindelwald*, and more recently produced *Mowgli: Legend of the Jungle*.

His additional credits include *Racing with the Moon*, *Wonder Boys*, *Flesh and Bone*, and *The Fabulous Baker Boys*. He also directed the latter two.

ALSO BY J.K. ROWLING

Harry Potter and the Sorcerer's Stone
Harry Potter and the Chamber of Secrets
Harry Potter and the Prisoner of Azkaban
Harry Potter and the Goblet of Fire
Harry Potter and the Order of the Phoenix
Harry Potter and the Half-Blood Prince
Harry Potter and the Deathly Hallows

Fantastic Beasts and Where to Find Them
Quidditch Through the Ages
(published in aid of Comic Relief and Lumos)

The Tales of Beedle the Bard
(published in aid of Lumos)

Harry Potter and the Cursed Child
(Based on an original story by J.K. Rowling, John Tiffany,
and Jack Thorne. A play by Jack Thorne.)

Fantastic Beasts and Where to Find Them (The Original Screenplay)
Fantastic Beasts: The Crimes of Grindelwald (The Original Screenplay)

The Ickabog
The Christmas Pig

Special thanks to the cast, crew, and creative team from *Fantastic Beasts: The Secrets of Dumbledore*, whose work is featured in the commentary, production renderings, sketches, and graphic designs included in this book.

This book was designed by Paul Kepple and Alex Bruce at Headcase Design. The text was set in ITC Stone Serif, a typeface designed by Sumner Stone.